Zicci by Edward Bulwer-Lytton

A Tale

Edward George Earle Bulwer-Lytton was born on May 25th, 1803 the youngest of three sons.

When Edward was four his father died and his mother moved the family to London. As a child he was delicate and neurotic and failed to fit in at any number of boarding schools. However, he was academically and creatively precocious and, as a teenager, he published his first work; Ishmael and Other Poems in 1820.

In 1822 he entered university at Cambridge and in 1825 he won the Chancellor's Gold Medal for English verse for Sculpture. The following year he received his B.A. degree and printed, for private circulation, the small volume of poems, Weeds and Wild Flowers.

During his career he was to be extremely prolific and write across a number of genres; historical fiction, mystery, romance, the occult, and science fiction as well as poetry.

In 1828 his novel, Pelham, brought him an income, as well as a commercial and critical reputation. The books intricate plot and humorous, intimate portrayals kept many a gossip busy trying to pair up public figures with characters in the book.

Bulwer-Lytton reached, perhaps, the height of his popularity with the publication of Godolphin (1833), followed by The Pilgrims of the Rhine (1834), The Last Days of Pompeii (1834), Rienzi, Last of the Roman Tribunes (1835), and Harold, the Last of the Saxons (1848).

In 1841, he started the Monthly Chronicle, a semi-scientific magazine. The Victorian era was filled with many magazines and periodicals all of whom had a great fascination to chronicle and publish the many things that the Empire and Industrial Revolution were discovering, inventing and changing.

In 1858 he entered Lord Derby's government as Secretary of State for the Colonies. He took an active interest in the development of the Crown Colony of British Columbia and wrote with great passion to the Royal Engineers upon assigning them their duties there.

In 1866 Bulwer-Lytton was raised to the peerage as Baron Lytton of Knebworth in the County of Hertford but his passion for politics now somewhat dimmed.

Bulwer-Lytton had long suffered with a disease of the ear and for the last two or three years of his life he lived in Torquay nursing his health. An operation to cure his deafness resulted in an abscess forming in his ear which later burst.

Edward George Earle Bulwer-Lytton endured intense pain for a week and died at 2am on January 18th, 1873, in Torquay, just short of his 70th birthday.

Index of Contents

BOOK I
Chapter I
Chapter II
Chapter III
Chapter IV
Chapter V
Chapter VI
Chapter VII
Chapter VIII
Chapter IX
Chapter X
Chapter XI
Chapter XII
Chapter XIII
Chapter XIV
Chapter XV
Chapter XVI
Chapter XVII
Chapter XVIII
BOOK II
Chapter I
Chapter II
EDWARD BULWER-LYTTON – A SHORT BIOGRAPHY
EDWARD BULWER-LYTTON – A CONCISE BIBLIOGRAPHY

BOOK I

CHAPTER I

In the gardens at Naples, one summer evening in the last century, some four or five gentlemen were seated under a tree drinking their sherbet and listening, in the intervals of conversation, to the music which enlivened that gay and favorite resort of an indolent population. One of this little party was a young Englishman who had been the life of the whole group, but who for the last few moments had sunk into a gloomy and abstracted revery. One of his countrymen observed this sudden gloom, and tapping him on the back, said, "Glyndon, why, what ails you? Are you ill? You have grown quite pale; you tremble: is it a sudden chill? You had better go home; these Italian nights are often dangerous to our English constitutions."

"No, I am well now,—it was but a passing shudder; I cannot account for it myself."

A man apparently of about thirty years of age, and of a mien and countenance strikingly superior to those around him, turned abruptly, and looked steadfastly at Glyndon.

"I think I understand what you mean," said he, "and perhaps," he added, with a grave smile, "I could explain it better than yourself." Here, turning to the others, he added, "You must often have felt, gentlemen,—each and all of you,—especially when sitting alone at night, a strange and unaccountable sensation of coldness and awe creep over you; your blood curdles, and the heart stands still; the limbs shiver, the hair bristles; you are afraid to look up, to turn your eyes to the darker corners of the room; you have a horrible fancy that something unearthly is at hand. Presently the whole spell, if I may so call it, passes away, and you are ready to laugh at your own weakness. Have you not often felt what I have thus imperfectly described? If so, you can understand what our young friend has just experienced, even amidst the delights of this magical scene, and amidst the balmy whispers of a July night."

"Sir," replied Glyndon, evidently much surprised, "you have defined exactly the nature of that shudder which came over me. But how could my manner be so faithful an index to my impressions?"

"I know the signs of the visitation," returned the stranger, gravely; "they are not to be mistaken by one of my experience."

All the gentlemen present then declared that they could comprehend, and had felt, what the stranger had described. "According to one of our national superstitions," said Merton, the Englishman who had first addressed Glyndon, "the moment you so feel your blood creep, and your hair stand on end, some one is walking over the spot which shall be your grave."

"There are in all lands different superstitions to account for so common an occurrence," replied the stranger; "one sect among the Arabians hold that at that instant God is deciding the hour either of your death or that of some one dear to you. The African savage, whose imagination is darkened by the hideous rites of his gloomy idolatry, believes that the Evil Spirit is pulling you towards him by the hair. So do the Grotesque and the Terrible mingle with each other."

"It is evidently a mere physical accident,—a derangement of the stomach; a chill of the blood," said a young Neapolitan.

"Then why is it always coupled, in all nations, with some superstitious presentiment or terror,—some connection between the material frame and the supposed world without us?" asked the stranger. "For my part, I think—"

"What do you think, sir?" asked Glyndon, curiously.

"I think," continued the stranger, "that it is the repugnance and horror of that which is human about us to something indeed invisible, but antipathetic to our own nature, and from a knowledge of which we are happily secured by the imperfection of our senses."

"You are a believer in spirits, then?" asked Merton, with an incredulous smile.

"Nay, I said not so. I can form no notion of a spirit, as the metaphysicians do, and certainly have no fear of one; but there may be forms of matter as invisible and impalpable to us as the animalculae to which I have compared them. The monster that lives and dies in a drop of water, carniverous, insatiable, subsisting on the creatures minuter than himself, is not less deadly in his wrath, less ferocious in his nature, than the tiger of the desert. There may be things around us malignant and hostile to men, if Providence had not placed a wall between them and us, merely by different modifications of matter."

"And could that wall never be removed?" asked young Glyndon, abruptly. "Are the traditions of sorcerer and wizard, universal and immemorial as they are, merely fables?"

"Perhaps yes; perhaps no," answered the stranger, indifferently. "But who, in an age in which the reason has chosen its proper bounds, would be mad enough to break the partition that divides him from the boa and the lion, to repine at and rebel against the law of nature which confines the shark to the great deep? Enough of these idle speculations."

Here the stranger rose, summoned the attendant, paid for his sherbet, and, bowing slightly to the company, soon disappeared among the trees.

"Who is that gentleman?" asked Glyndon, eagerly.

The rest looked at each other, without replying, for some moments.

"I never saw him before," said Merton, at last.

"Nor I."

"Nor I."

"I have met him often," said the Neapolitan, who was named Count Cetoxa; "it was, if you remember, as my companion that he joined you. He has been some months at Naples; he is very rich,—indeed enormously so. Our acquaintance commenced in a strange way."

"How was it?"

"I had been playing at a public gaming-house, and had lost considerably. I rose from the table, resolved no longer to tempt Fortune, when this gentleman, who had hitherto been a spectator, laying his hand on my arm, said with politeness, 'Sir, I see you enjoy play,—I dislike it; but I yet wish to have some interest in what is going on. Will you play this sum for me? The risk is mine,—the half-profits yours.' I was startled, as you may suppose, at such an address; but the stranger had an air and tone with him it was impossible to resist. Besides, I was burning to recover my losses, and should not have risen had I had any money left about me. I told him I would accept his offer, provided we shared the risk as well as profits. 'As you will,' said he, smiling, 'we need have no scruple, for you will be sure to win.' I sat down, the stranger stood behind me; my luck rose, I invariably won. In fact, I rose from the table a rich man."

"There can be no foul play at the public tables, especially when foul play would make against the bank."

"Certainly not," replied the count. "But our good fortune was indeed marvellous,—so extraordinary that a Sicilian (the Sicilians are all ill-bred, bad-tempered fellows) grew angry and insolent. 'Sir,' said he, turning to my new friend, 'you have no business to stand so near to the table. I do not understand this; you have not acted fairly.' The spectator replied, with great composure, that he had done nothing against the rules; that he was very sorry that one man could not win without another man losing; and that he could not act unfairly even if disposed to do so. The Sicilian took the stranger's mildness for apprehension,—blustered more loudly, and at length fairly challenged him. 'I never seek a quarrel, and I never shun a danger,' returned my partner; and six or seven of us adjourned to the garden behind the house. I was of course my partner's second. He took me aside. 'This man will die,' said he; 'see that he is buried privately in the church of St. Januario, by the side of his father.'

"'Did you know his family?' I asked with great surprise. He made no answer, but drew his sword and walked deliberately to the spot we had selected. The Sicilian was a renowned swordsman; nevertheless, in the third pass he was run through the body. I went up to him; he could scarcely speak. 'Have you any request to make,—any affairs to settle?' He shook his head. 'Where would you wish to be interred?' He pointed towards the Sicilian coast. 'What!' said I, in surprise, 'not by the side of your father?' As I spoke, his face altered terribly, he uttered a piercing shriek; the blood gushed from his mouth, and he fell dead. The most strange part of the story is to come. We buried him in the church of St. Januario. In doing so, we took up his father's coffin; the lid came off in moving it, and the skeleton was visible. In the hollow of the skull we found a very slender wire of sharp steel; this caused great surprise and inquiry. The father, who was rich and a miser, had died suddenly and been buried in haste, owing, it was said, to the heat of the weather. Suspicion once awakened, the examination became minute. The old man's servant was questioned, and at last confessed that the son had murdered the sire. The contrivance was ingenious; the wire was so slender that it pierced to the brain and drew but one drop of blood, which the gray hairs concealed. The accomplice was executed."

"And this stranger, did he give evidence? Did he account for—"

"No," interrupted the count, "he declared that he had by accident visited the church that morning; that he had observed the tombstone of the Count Salvolio; that his guide had told him the count's son was in Naples,—a spendthrift and a gambler. While we were at play, he had heard the count mentioned by name at the table; and when the challenge was given and accepted, it had occured to him to name the place of burial, by an instinct he could not account for."

"A very lame story," said Merton.

"Yes, but we Italians are superstitious. The alleged instinct was regarded as the whisper of Providence; the stranger became an object of universal interest and curiosity. His wealth, his manner of living, his extraordinary personal beauty, have assisted also to make him the rage."

"What is his name?" asked Glyndon.

"Zicci. Signor Zicci."

"Is it not an Italian name? He speaks English like a native."

"So he does French and German, as well as Italian, to my knowledge. But he declares himself a Corsican by birth, though I cannot hear of any eminent Corsican family of that name. However, what matters his birth or parentage? He is rich, generous, and the best swordsman I ever saw in my life. Who would affront him?"

"Not I, certainly," said Merton, rising. "Come, Glyndon, shall we seek our hotel? It is almost daylight. Adieu, signor."

"What think you of this story?" said Glyndon as the young men walked homeward.

"Why, it is very clear that this Zicci is some impostor, some clever rogue; and the Neapolitan shares booty, and puffs him off with all the hackneyed charlatanism of the marvellous. An unknown adventurer gets into society by being made an object of awe and curiosity; he is devilish handsome; and the women are quite content to receive him without any other recommendation than his own face and Cetoxa's fables."

"I cannot agree with you. Cetoxa, though a gambler and a rake, is a nobleman of birth and high repute for courage and honor. Besides, this stranger, with his grand features and lofty air,—so calm, so unobtrusive,—has nothing in common with the forward garrulity of an impostor."

"My dear Glyndon, pardon me, but you have not yet acquired any knowledge of the world; the stranger makes the best of a fine person, and his grand air is but a trick of the trade. But to change the subject: how gets on the love affair?"

"Oh! Isabel could not see me to-night. The old woman gave me a note of excuse."

"You must not marry her; what would they all say at home?"

"Let us enjoy the present," said Glyndon, with vivacity; "we are young, rich, good-looking: let us not think of to-morrow."

"Bravo, Glyndon! Here we are at the hotel. Sleep sound, and don't dream of Signor Zicci."

CHAPTER II

Clarence Glyndon was a young man of small but independent fortune. He had, early in life, evinced considerable promise in the art of painting, and rather from enthusiasm than the want of a profession, he had resolved to devote himself to a career which in England has been seldom entered upon by persons who can live on their own means. Without being a poet, Glyndon had also manifested a graceful faculty for verse, which had contributed to win his entry into society above his birth. Spoiled and flattered from his youth upward, his natural talents were in some measure relaxed by indolence and that worldly and selfish habit of thought which frivolous companionship often engenders, and which is withering alike to stern virtue and high genius. The luxuriance of his fancy was unabated; but the affections, which are the life of fancy, had grown languid and inactive. His youth, his vanity, and a restless daring and thirst of adventure had from time to time involved him in dangers and dilemmas, out of which, of late, he had always extricated himself with the ingenious felicity of a clever head and cool heart. He had left England for Rome with the avowed purpose and sincere resolution of studying the divine masterpieces of art; but pleasure had soon allured him from ambition, and he quitted the gloomy palaces of Rome for the gay shores and animated revelries of Naples. Here he had fallen in love—deeply in love, as he said and thought—with a young person celebrated at Naples, Isabel di Pisani. She was the only daughter of an Italian by an English mother. The father had known better days; in his prosperity he had travelled, and won in England the affections of a lady of some fortune. He had been induced to speculate; he lost his all; he settled at Naples, and taught languages and music. His wife died when Isabel, christened from her mother, was ten years old. At sixteen she came out on the stage; two years afterwards her father departed this life, and Isabel was an orphan.

Glyndon, a man of pleasure and a regular attendant at the theatre, had remarked the young actress behind the scenes; he fell in love with her, and he told her so. The girl listened to him, perhaps from vanity, perhaps from ambition, perhaps from coquetry; she listened, and allowed but few stolen interviews, in which she permitted no favor to the Englishman it was one reason why he loved her so much.

The day following that on which our story opens, Glyndon was riding alone by the shores of the Neapolitan sea, on the other side of the Cavern of Pausilippo. It was past noon; the sun had lost its early fervor, and a cool breeze sprang voluptuously from the sparkling sea. Bending over a fragment of stone near the roadside, he perceived the form of a man; and when he approached he recognized Zicci.

The Englishman saluted him courteously. "Have you discovered some antique?" said he, with a smile; "they are as common as pebbles on this road."

"No," replied Zicci; "it was but one of those antiques that have their date, indeed, from the beginning of the world, but which Nature eternally withers and renews." So saying, he showed Glyndon a small herb with a pale blue flower, and then placed it carefully in his bosom.

"You are an herbalist?"

"I am."

"It is, I am told, a study full of interest."

"To those who understand it, doubtless. But," continued Zicci, looking up with a slight and cold smile, "why do you linger on your way to converse with me on matters in which you neither have knowledge nor desire to obtain it? I read your heart, young Englishman: your curiosity is excited; you wish to know me, and not this humble herb. Pass on; your desire never can be satisfied."

"You have not the politeness of your countrymen," said Glyndon, somewhat discomposed. "Suppose I were desirous to cultivate your acquaintance, why should you reject my advances?"

"I reject no man's advances," answered Zicci. "I must know them, if they so desire; but me, in return, they can never comprehend. If you ask my acquaintance, it is yours; but I would warn you to shun me."

"And why are you then so dangerous?"

"Some have found me so; if I were to predict your fortune by the vain calculations of the astrologer, I should tell you, in their despicable jargon, that my planet sat darkly in your house of life. Cross me not, if you can avoid it. I warn you now for the first time and last."

"You despise the astrologers, yet you utter a jargon as mysterious as theirs. I neither gamble nor quarrel: why then should I fear you?"

"As you will; I have done."

"Let me speak frankly: your conversation last night interested and amused me."

"I know it; minds like yours are attracted by mystery."

Glyndon was piqued at those words, though in the tone in which they were spoken there was no contempt.

"I see you do not consider me worthy of your friendship be it so. Good day."

Zicci coldly replied to the salutation, and as the Englishman rode on, returned to his botanical employment.

The same night Glyndon went, as usual, to the theatre. He was standing behind the scenes watching Isabel, who was on the stage in one of her most brilliant parts. The house resounded with applause. Glyndon was transported with a young man's passion and a young man's pride. "This glorious creature," thought he, "may yet be mine."

He felt, while thus rapt in delicious revery, a slight touch upon his shoulder; he turned, and beheld Zicci. "You are in danger," said the latter. "Do not walk home to-night; or if you do, go not alone."

Before Glyndon recovered from his surprise, Zicci disappeared; and when the Englishman saw him again, he was in the box of one of the Neapolitan ministers, where Glyndon could not follow him.

Isabel now left the stage, and Glyndon accosted her with impassioned gallantry. The actress was surprisingly beautiful; of fair complexion and golden hair, her countenance was relieved from the tame and gentle loveliness which the Italians suppose to be the characteristics of English beauty, by the contrast of dark eyes and lashes, by a forehead of great height, to which the dark outline of the eyebrows gave some thing of majesty and command. In spite of the slightness of virgin youth, her proportions had the nobleness, blent with the delicacy, that belongs to the masterpieces of ancient sculpture; and there was a conscious pride in her step, and in the swanlike bend of her stately head, as she turned with an evident impatience from the address of her lover. Taking aside an old woman, who was her constant and confidential attendant at the theatre, she said, in an earnest whisper,—

"Oh, Gionetta, he is here again! I have seen him again! And again, he alone of the whole theatre withholds from me his applause. He scarcely seems to notice me; his indifference mortifies me to the soul,—I could weep for rage and sorrow."

"Which is he, my darling?" said the old woman, with fondness in her voice. "He must be dull,—not worth thy thoughts."

The actress drew Gionetta nearer to the stage, and pointed out to her a man in one of the nearer boxes, conspicuous amongst all else by the simplicity of his dress and the extraordinary beauty of his features.

"Not worth a thought, Gionetta," repeated Isabel,—"not worth a thought! Saw you ever one so noble, so godlike?"

"By the Holy Mother!" answered Gionetta, "he is a proper man, and has the air of a prince."

The prompter summoned the Signora Pisani. "Find out his name, Gionetta," said she, sweeping on to the stage, and passing by Glyndon, who gazed at her with a look of sorrowful reproach.

The scene on which the actress now entered was that of the final catastrophe, wherein all her remarkable powers of voice and art were pre-eminently called forth. The house hung on every word with breathless worship, but the eyes of Isabel sought only those of one calm and unmoved spectator; she exerted herself as if inspired. The stranger listened, and observed her with an attentive gaze, but no approval escaped his lips, no emotion changed the expression of his cold and half-disdainful aspect. Isabel, who was in the character of a jealous and abandoned mistress, never felt so acutely the part she played. Her tears were truthful; her passion that of nature: it was almost too terrible to behold. She was borne from the stage, exhausted and insensible, amidst such a tempest of admiring rapture as Continental audiences alone can raise. The crowd stood up, handkerchiefs waved, garlands and flowers were thrown on the stage, men wiped their eyes, and women sobbed aloud.

"By heavens!" said a Neapolitan of great rank, "she has fired me beyond endurance. To-night, this very night, she shall be mine! You have arranged all, Mascari?"

"All, signor. And if this young Englishman should accompany her home?"

"The presuming barbarian! At all events let him bleed for his folly. I hear that she admits him to secret interviews. I will have no rival."

"But an Englishman! There is always a search after the bodies of the English."

"Fool! Is not the sea deep enough, or the earth secret enough, to hide one dead man? Our ruffians are silent as the grave itself. And I,—who would dare to suspect, to arraign, the Prince di—? See to it,—let him be watched, and the fitting occasion taken. I trust him to you,—robbers murder him; you understand: the country swarms with them. Plunder and strip him. Take three men; the rest shall be my escort."

Mascari shrugged his shoulders, and bowed submissively. Meanwhile Glyndon besought Isabel, who recovered but slowly, to return home in his carriage. (1) She had done so once or twice before, though she had never permitted him to accompany her. This time she refused, and with some petulance. Glyndon, offended, was retiring sullenly, when Gionetta stopped him. "Stay, signor," said she, coaxingly, "the dear signora is not well: do not be angry with her; I will make her accept your offer."

Glyndon stayed, and after a few moments spent in expostulation on the part of Gionetta, and resistance on that of Isabel, the offer was accepted; the actress, with a mixture of naivete and coquetry, gave her handy to her lover, who kissed it with delight. Gionetta and her charge entered the carriage, and Glyndon was left at the door of the theatre, to return home on foot. The mysterious warning of Zicci then suddenly occurred to him; he had forgotten it in the interest of his lover's quarrel with Isabel. He thought it now advisable to guard against danger foretold by lips so mysterious; he looked round for some one he knew. The theatre was disgorging its crowds, who hustled and jostled and pressed upon him; but he recognized no familiar countenances. While pausing irresolute, he heard Merton's voice calling on him, and to his great relief discovered his friend making his way through the throng.

"I have secured you a place in the Count Cetoxa's carriage," said he. "Come along, he is waiting for us."

"How kind in you! How did you find me out?"

"I met Zicci in the passage. 'Your friend is at the door of the theatre,' said he; 'do not let him go home alone to-night the streets of Naples are not always safe.' I immediately remembered that some of the Calabrian bravos had been busy within the city the last few weeks, and asked Cetoxa, who was with me, to accompany you."

Further explanation was forbidden, for they now joined the count. As Glyndon entered the carriage and drew up the glass, he saw four men standing apart by the pavement, who seemed to eye him with attention.

"Cospetto!" cried one; "ecco Inglese!" Glyndon imperfectly heard the exclamation as the carriage drove on. He reached home in safety.

"Have you discovered who he is?" asked the actress, as she was now alone in the carriage with Gionetta.

"Yes, he is the celebrated Signor Zicci, about whom the court has run mad. They say he is so rich,—oh, so much richer than any of the Inglese! But a bird in the hand, my angel, is better than—"

"Cease," interrupted the young actress. "Zicci! Speak of the Englishman no more."

The carriage was now entering that more lonely and remote part of the city in which Isabel's house was situated, when it suddenly stopped.

Gionetta, in alarm, thrust her head out of window, and perceived by the pale light of the moon that the driver, torn from his seat, was already pinioned in the arms of two men; the next moment the door was opened violently, and a tall figure, masked and mantled, appeared.

"Fear not, fairest Pisani," said he, gently, "no ill shall befall you." As he spoke, he wound his arms round the form of the fair actress, and endeavored to lift her from the carriage. But the Signora Pisani was not an ordinary person; she had been before exposed to all the dangers to which the beauty of the low-born was subjected amongst a lawless and profligate nobility. She thrust back the assailant with a power that surprised him, and in the next moment the blade of a dagger gleamed before his eyes. "Touch me," said she, drawing herself to the farther end of the carriage, "and I strike!"

The mask drew back.

"By the body of Bacchus, a bold spirit!" said he, half laughing and half alarmed. "Here, Luigi, Giovanni! disarm and seize her. Harm her not."

The mask retired from the door, and another and yet taller form presented itself. "Be calm, Isabel di Pisani," said he, in a low voice; "with me you are indeed safe!" He lifted his mask as he spoke, and showed the noble features of Zicci. "Be calm, be hushed; I can save you." He vanished, leaving Isabel lost in surprise, agitation, and delight. There were in all nine masks: two were engaged with the driver; one stood at the head of the carriage-horses; a third guarded the well-trained steeds of the party; three others, besides Zicci and the one who had first accosted Isabel, stood apart by a carriage drawn to the side of the road. To these Zicci motioned: they advanced; he pointed towards the first mask, who was in fact the Prince di—, and to his unspeakable astonishment the Prince was suddenly seized from behind.

"Treason," he cried, "treason among my own men! What means this?"

"Place him in his carriage. If he resist, shoot him!" said Zicci, calmly.

He approached the men who had detained the coachman. "You are outnumbered and outwitted," said he. "Join your lord; you are three men,—we six, armed to the teeth. Thank our mercy that we spare your lives. Go!"

The men gave way, dismayed. The driver remounted. "Cut the traces of their carriage and the bridles of their horses," said Zicci, as he entered the vehicle containing Isabel, and which now drove on rapidly, leaving the discomfited ravisher in a state of rage and stupor impossible to describe.

"Allow me to explain this mystery to you," said Zicci. "I discovered the plot against you,—no matter how. I frustrated it thus: the head of this design is a nobleman who has long persecuted you in vain. He and two of his creatures watched you from the entrance of the theatre, having directed six others to await him on the spot where you were attacked; myself and five of my servants supplied their place, and were mistaken for his own followers. I had previously ridden alone to the spot where the men were waiting, and informed them that their master would not require their services that night. They believed me, for I showed them his signet-ring, and accordingly dispersed; I then joined my own band, whom I had left in the rear. You know all. We are at your door."

(1) At that time in Naples carriages were both cheaper to hire, and more necessary for strangers than they are now.

CHAPTER III

Zicci was left alone with the young Italian. She had thrown aside her cloak and head-gear; her hair, somewhat dishevelled, fell down her ivory neck, which the dress partially displayed; she seemed, as she sat in that low and humble chamber, a very vision of light and glory.

Zicci gazed at her with an admiration mingled with compassion; he muttered a few words to himself, and then addressed her aloud:—

"Isabel di Pisani, I have saved you from a great peril,—not from dishonor only, but perhaps from death. The Prince di—, under the weak government of a royal child and a venal administration, is a man above the law. He is capable of every crime; but amongst his passions he has such prudence as belongs to ambition: if you were not to reconcile yourself to your shame, you would never enter the world again to tell your tale. The ravisher has no heart for repentance, but he has a hand that can murder. I have saved thee, Isabel di Pisani. Perhaps you would ask me wherefore?" Zicci paused, and smiled mournfully as he added: "My life is not that of others, but I am still human,—I know pity; and more, Isabel, I can feel gratitude for affection. You love me; it was my fate to fascinate your eye, to arouse your vanity, to inflame your imagination. It was to warn you from this folly that I consented for a few minutes to become your guest. The Englishman, Glyndon, loves thee well,—better than I can ever love; he may wed thee, he may bear thee to his own free and happy land,—the land of thy mother's kin. Forget me, teach thyself to return and to deserve his love; and I tell thee that thou wilt be honored and be happy."

Isabel listened with silent wonder and deep blushes to this strange address; and when the voice ceased, she covered her face with her hands and wept.

Zicci rose. "I have fulfilled my duty to you, and I depart. Remember that you are still in danger from the prince; be wary, and be cautious. Your best precaution is in flight; farewell."

"Oh, do not leave me yet! You have read a secret of which I myself was scarcely conscious: you despise me,—you, my preserver! Ah! do not misjudge me; I am better, higher than I seem. Since I saw thee I have been a new being." The poor girl clasped her hands passionately as she spoke, and her tears streamed down her cheeks.

"What would you that I should answer?" said Zicci, pausing, but with a cold severity in his eye.

"Say that you do not despise,—say that you do not think me light and shameless."

"Willingly, Isabel. I know your heart and your history you are capable of great virtues; you have the seeds of a rare and powerful genius. You may pass through the brief period of your human life with a proud step and a cheerful heart, if you listen to my advice. You have been neglected from your childhood; you have been thrown among nations at once frivolous and coarse; your nobler dispositions, your higher qualities, are not developed. You were pleased with the admiration of Glyndon; you thought that the passionate stranger might marry you, while others had only uttered the vows that dishonor. Poor child, it was the instinctive desire of right within thee that made thee listen to him; and if my fatal shadow had not crossed thy path, thou wouldst have loved him well enough, at least, for content. Return to that hope, and nurse again that innocent affection: this is my answer to thee. Art thou contented?"

"No! ah, no! Severe as thou art, I love better to hear thee than, than—What am I saying? And now you have saved me, I shall pray for you, bless you, think of you; and am I never to see you more? Alas! the moment you leave me, danger and dread will darken round me. Let me be your servant, your slave; with you I should have no fear."

A dark shade fell over Zicci's brow; he looked from the ground, on which his eyes had rested while she spoke, upon the earnest and imploring face of the beautiful creature that now knelt before him, with all the passions of an ardent and pure, but wholly untutored and half-savage, nature speaking from the tearful eyes and trembling lips. He looked at her with an aspect she could not interpret; in his eyes were kindness, sorrow, and even something, she thought, of love: yet the brow frowned, and the lip was stern.

"It is in vain that we struggle with our doom," said he, calmly; "listen to me yet. I am a man, Isabel, in whom there are some good impulses yet left, but whose life is, on the whole, devoted to a systematic and selfish desire to enjoy whatever life can afford. To me it is given to warn: the warning neglected, I interfere no more; I leave her victories to that Fate that I cannot baffle of her prey. You do not understand me; no matter: what I am now about to say will be more easy to comprehend. I tell thee to tear from thy heart all thought of me: thou hast yet the power. If thou wilt not obey me, thou must reap the seeds that thou wilt sow. Glyndon, if thou acceptest his homage, will love thee throughout life; I, too, can love thee."

"You, you—"

"But with a lukewarm and selfish love, and one that cannot last. Thou wilt be a flower in my path; I inhale thy sweetness and pass on, caring not what wind shall sup thee, or what step shall tread thee to the dust. Which is the love thou wouldst prefer?"

"But do you, can you love me,—you, you, Zicci,—even for an hour? Say it again."

"Yes, Isabel; I am not dead to beauty, and yours is that rarely given to the daughters of men. Yes, Isabel, I could love thee!"

Isabel uttered a cry of joy, seized his hand, and kissed it through burning and impassioned tears. Zicci raised her in his arms and imprinted one kiss upon her forehead.

"Do not deceive thyself," he said; "consider well. I tell thee again that my love is subjected to the certain curse of change. For my part, I shall seek thee no more. Thy fate shall be thine own, and not mine. For the rest, fear not the Prince di—. At present, I can save thee from every harm." With these words he withdrew himself from her embrace, and had gained the outer door just as Gionetta came from the kitchen with her hands full of such cheer as she had managed to collect together. Zicci laid his hand on the old woman's arm.

"Signor Glyndon," said he, "loves Isabel; he may wed her. You love your mistress: plead for him. Disabuse her, if you can, of any caprice for me. I am a bird ever on the wing." He dropped a purse, heavy with gold, into Gionetta's bosom, and was gone.

CHAPTER IV

The palace of Zicci was among the noblest in Naples. It still stands, though ruined and dismantled, in one of those antique streets from which the old races of the Norman and the Spaniard have long since vanished.

He ascended the vast staircase, and entered the rooms reserved for his private hours. They were no wise remarkable except for their luxury and splendor, and the absence of what men so learned as Zicci was reputed, generally prize, namely, books. Zicci seemed to know everything that books can teach; yet of books themselves he spoke and thought with the most profound contempt.

He threw himself on a sofa, and dismissed his attendants for the night; and here it may be observed that Zicci had no one servant who knew anything of his origin, birth, or history. Some of his attendants he had brought with him from other cities; the rest he had engaged at Naples. He hired those only whom wealth can make subservient. His expenditure was most lavish, his generosity, regal; but his orders were ever given as those of a general to his army. The least disobedience, the least hesitation, and the offender was at once dismissed. He was a man who sought tools, and never made confidants.

Zicci remained for a considerable time motionless and thoughtful. The hand of the clock before him pointed to the first hour of morning. The solemn voice of the timepiece aroused him from his revery.

"One sand more out of the mighty hour-glass," said he, rising; "one hour nearer to the last! I am weary of humanity. I will enter into one of the countless worlds around me." He lifted the arras that clothed the walls, and touching a strong iron door (then made visible) with a minute key which he wore in a ring, passed into an inner apartment lighted by a single lamp of extraordinary lustre. The room was small; a few phials and some dried herbs were ranged in shelves on the wall, which was hung with snow-white cloth of coarse texture. From the shelves Zicci selected one of the phials, and poured the contents into a crystal cup. The liquid was colorless, and sparkled rapidly up in bubbles of light; it almost seemed to evaporate ere it reached his lips. But when the strange beverage was quaffed, a sudden change was visible in the countenance of Zicci: his beauty became yet more dazzling, his eyes shone with intense fire, and his form seemed to grow more youthful and ethereal.

CHAPTER V

The next day, Glyndon bent his steps towards Zicci's palace. The young man's imagination, naturally inflammable, was singularly excited by the little he had seen and heard of this strange being; a spell he could neither master nor account for, attracted him towards the stranger. Zicci's power seemed mysterious and great, his motives kindly and benevolent, yet his manners chilling and repellant. Why at one moment reject Glyndon's acquaintance, at another save him from danger? How had Zicci thus acquired the knowledge of enemies unknown to Glyndon himself? His interest was deeply roused, his gratitude appealed to; he resolved to make another effort to conciliate Zicci.

The signor was at home, and Glyndon was admitted into a lofty saloon, where in a few moments Zicci joined him.

"I am come to thank you for your warning last night," said he, "and to entreat you to complete my obligation by informing me of the quarter to which I may look for enmity and peril."

"You are a gallant, Mr. Glyndon," said Zicci, with a smile; "and do you know so little of the South as not to be aware that gallants have always rivals?"

"Are you serious?" said Glyndon, coloring.

"Most serious. You love Isabel di Pisani; you have for rival one of the most powerful and relentless of the Neapolitan princes. Your danger is indeed great."

"But, pardon me, how came it known to you?"

"I give no account of myself to mortal man," replied Zicci, haughtily; "and to me it matters not whether you regard or scorn my warning."

"Well, if I may not question you, be it so; but at least advise me what to do."

"You will not follow my advice."

"You wrong me! Why?"

"Because you are constitutionally brave; you are fond of excitement and mystery; you like to be the hero of a romance. I should advise you to leave Naples, and you will disdain to do so while Naples contains a foe to shun or a mistress to pursue."

"You are right," said the young Englishman, with energy; "and you cannot reproach me for such a resolution."

"No, there is another course left to you. Do you love Isabel di Pisani truly and fervently? If so, marry her, and take a bride to your native land."

"Nay," answered Glyndon, embarrassed. "Isabel is not of my rank; her character is strange and self-willed; her education neglected. I am enslaved by her beauty, but I cannot wed her."

Zicci frowned.

"Your love, then, is but selfish lust; and by that love you will be betrayed. Young man, Destiny is less inexorable than it appears. The resources of the great Ruler of the Universe are not so scanty and so stern as to deny to men the divine privilege of Free Will; all of us can carve out our own way, and God can make our very contradictions harmonize with His solemn ends. You have before you an option. Honorable and generous love may even now work out your happiness and effect your escape; a frantic and interested passion will but lead you to misery and doom."

"Do you pretend, then, to read the Future?"

"I have said all that it pleases me to utter."

"While you assume the moralist to me, Signor Zicci," said Glyndon, with a smile, "if report says true you do not yourself reject the allurements of unfettered love."

"If it were necessary that practice square with precept," said Zicci, with a sneer, "our pulpits would be empty. Do you think it matters, in the great aggregate of human destinies, what one man's conduct may be? Nothing,—not a grain of dust; but it matters much what are the sentiments he propagates. His acts are limited and momentary; his sentiments may pervade the universe, and inspire generations till the day of doom. All our virtues, all our laws, are drawn from books and maxims, which are sentiments, not from deeds. Our opinions, young Englishman, are the angel part of us; our acts the earthly."

"You have reflected deeply, for an Italian," said Glyndon.

"Who told you I was an Italian?"

"Are you not of Corsica?"

"Tush!" said Zicci, impatiently turning away. Then, after a pause, he resumed, in a mild voice: "Glyndon, do you renounce Isabel di Pisani? Will you take three days to consider of what I have said?"

"Renounce her,—never!"

"Then you will marry her?"

"Impossible."

"Be it so; she will then renounce you. I tell you that you have rivals."

"Yes, the Prince di—; but I do not fear him."

"You have another, whom you will fear more."

"And who is he?"

"Myself."

Glyndon turned pale, and started from his seat.

"You, Signor Zicci, you,—and you dare to tell me so?"

"Dare! Alas! you know there is nothing on earth left me to fear!"

These words were not uttered arrogantly, but in a tone of the most mournful dejection. Glyndon was enraged, confounded, and yet awed. However, he had a brave English heart within his breast, and he recovered himself quickly.

"Signor," said he, calmly, "I am not to be duped by these solemn phrases and these mystical sympathies. You may have power which I cannot comprehend or emulate, or you may be but a keen impostor."

"Well, sir, your logical position is not ill-taken; proceed."

"I mean then," continued Glyndon, resolutely, though somewhat disconcerted, "I mean you to understand, that, though I am not to be persuaded or compelled by a stranger to marry Isabel di Pisani, I am not the less determined never tamely to yield her to another."

Zicci looked gravely at the young man, whose sparkling eyes and heightened color testified the spirit to support his words, and replied: "So bold! well, it becomes you. You have courage, then; I thought it. Perhaps it may be put to a sharper test than you dream of. But take my advice: wait three days, and tell me then if you will marry this young person."

"But if you love her, why, why—"

"Why am I anxious that she should wed another? To save her from myself! Listen to me. That girl, humble and uneducated though she be, has in her the seeds of the most lofty qualities and virtues. She can be all to the man she loves,—all that man can desire in wife or mistress. Her soul, developed by affection, will elevate your own; it will influence your fortunes, exalt your destiny; you will become a great and prosperous man. If, on the contrary, she fall to me, I know not what may be her lot; but I know that few can pass the ordeal, and hitherto no woman has survived the struggle."

As Zicci spoke, his face became livid, and there was something in his voice that froze the warm blood of his listener.

"What is this mystery which surrounds you?" exclaimed Glyndon, unable to repress his emotion. "Are you, in truth, different from other men? Have you passed the boundary of lawful knowledge? Are you, as some declare, a sorcerer, only a—"

"Hush!" interrupted Zicci, gently, and with a smile of singular but melancholy sweetness: "have you earned the right to ask me these questions? The clays of torture and persecution are over; and a man may live as he pleases, and talk as it suits him, without fear of the stake and the rack. Since I can defy persecution, pardon me if I do not succumb to curiosity."

Glyndon blushed, and rose. In spite of his love for Isabel, and his natural terror of such a rival, he felt himself irresistibly drawn towards the very man he had most cause to suspect and dread. It was like the fascination of the basilisk. He held out his hand to Zicci, saying, "Well, then, if we are to be rivals, our swords must settle our rights; till then I would fain be friends."

"Friends! Pardon me, I like you too well to give you my friendship. You know not what you ask."

"Enigmas again!"

"Enigmas!" cried Zicci, passionately, "Nay: can you dare to solve them! Would you brave all that human heart can conceive of peril and of horror, so that you at last might stand separated from this visible universe side by side with me? When you can dare this, and when you are fit to dare it, I may give you my right hand and call you friend."

"I could dare everything and all things for the attainment of superhuman wisdom," said Glyndon; and his countenance was lighted up with wild and intense enthusiasm.

Zicci observed him in thoughtful silence.

"He may be worthy," he muttered; "he may, yet—" He broke off abruptly; then, speaking aloud, "Go, Glyndon," said he; "in three days we shall meet again."

"Where?"

"Perhaps where you can least anticipate. In any case, we shall meet."

CHAPTER VI

Glyndon thought seriously and deeply over all that the mysterious Zicci had said to him relative to Isabel. His imagination was inflamed by the vague and splendid promises that were connected with his marriage with the poor actress. His fears, too, were naturally aroused by the threat that by marriage alone could he save himself from the rivalry of Zicci,—Zicci, born to dazzle and command; Zicci, who united to the apparent wealth of a monarch the beauty of a god; Zicci, whose eye seemed to foresee, whose hand to frustrate, every danger. What a rival, and what a foe!

But Glyndon's pride, as well as jealousy, was aroused. He was brave comme son epee. Should he shrink from the power or the enmity of a man mortal as himself? And why should Zicci desire him to give his name and station to one of a calling so equivocal? Might there not be motives he could not fathom? Might not the actress and the Corsican be in league with each other? Might not all this jargon of prophecy—and menace be but artifices to dupe him,—the tool, perhaps, of a mountebank and his mistress! Mistress,—ah, no! If ever maidenhood wrote its modest characters externally, that pure eye, that noble forehead, that mien and manner so ingenuous even in their coquetry, their pride, assured him that Isabel was not the base and guilty thing he had dared for a moment to suspect her. Lost in a labyrinth of doubts and surmises, Glyndon turned on the practical sense of the sober Merton to assist and enlighten him.

As may be well supposed, his friend listened to his account of his interview with Zicci with a half-suppressed and ironical smile.

"Excellent, my dear friend! This Zicci is another Apollonius of Tyana,—nothing less will satisfy you. What! is it possible that you are the Clarence Glyndon of whose career such glowing hopes are entertained,—you the man whose genius has been extolled by all the graybeards? Not a boy turned out from a village school but would laugh you to scorn. And so because Signor Zicci tells you that you will be a marvellously great man if you revolt all your friends and blight all your prospects by marrying a Neapolitan actress, you begin already to think of—By Jupiter! I cannot talk patiently on the subject. Let the girl alone,—that would be the proper plan; or else—"

"You talk very sensibly," interrupted Glyndon, "but you distract me. I will go to Isabel's house; I will see her; I will judge for myself."

"That is certainly the best way to forget her," said Merton. Glyndon seized his hat and sword, and was gone.

CHAPTER VII

She was seated outside her door, the young actress. The sea, which in that heavenly bay literally seems to sleep in the arms of the shore, bounded the view in front; while to the right, not far off, rose the dark and tangled crags to which the traveller of to-day is daily brought to gaze on the tomb of Virgil, or compare with the Cavern of Pausilippo the archway of Highgate Hill. There were a few fishermen loitering by the cliffs, on which their nets were hung up to dry; and, at a distance, the sound of some rustic pipe (more common at that day than in this), mingled now and then with the bells of the lazy mules, broke the voluptuous silence,—the silence of declining noon on the shores of Naples. Never till you have enjoyed it, never till you have felt its enervating but delicious charm, believe that you can comprehend all the meaning of the dolce far niente; and when that luxury has been known, when you have breathed the atmosphere of fairy land, then you will no longer wonder why the heart ripens with so sudden and wild a power beneath the rosy skies and amidst the glorious foliage of the South.

The young actress was seated by the door of her house; overhead a rude canvas awning sheltered her from the sun; on her lap lay the manuscript of a new part in which she was shortly to appear. By her side was the guitar on which she had been practising the airs that were to ravish the ears of the cognoscenti. But the guitar had been thrown aside in despair; her voice this morning did not obey her will. The manuscript lay unheeded, and the eyes of the actress were fixed on the broad, blue deep beyond. In the unwonted negligence of her dress might be traced the abstraction of her mind. Her beautiful hair was gathered up loosely, and partially bandaged by a kerchief, whose purple color seemed to deepen the golden hue of the tresses. A stray curl escaped, and fell down the graceful neck. A loose morning robe, girded by a sash, left the breeze that came ever and anon from the sea to die upon the bust half disclosed, and the tiny slipper, that Cinderella might have worn, seemed a world too wide for the tiny foot which it scarcely covered. It might be the heat of the day that deepened the soft bloom of the cheeks and gave an unwonted languor to the large dark eyes. In all the pomp of her stage attire, in all the flush of excitement before the intoxicating lamps, never had Isabel looked so lovely.

By the side of the actress, and filling up the threshold, stood Gionetta, with her hands thrust up to the elbow in two huge recesses on either side her gown,—pockets, indeed, they might be called by courtesy; such pockets as Beelzebub's grandmother might have shaped for herself, bottomless pits in miniature.

"But I assure you," said the nurse, in that sharp, quick, earsplitting tone in which the old women of the South are more than a match for those of the North,—"but I assure you, my darling, that there is not a finer cavalier in all Naples, nor a more beautiful, than this Inglese; and I am told that all the Inglesi are much richer than they seem. Though they have no trees in their country, poor people, and instead of twenty-four they have only twelve hours to the day, yet I hear, cospetto! that they shoe their horses with steak; and since they cannot (the poor heretics!) turn grapes into wine, for they have no grapes, they turn gold into physic, and take a glass or two of pistoles whenever they are troubled with the colic. But you don't hear me! Little pupil of my eyes, you don't hear me!"

"Gionetta, is he not god-like?"

"Sancta Maria! he is handsome, bellissimo; and when you are his wife,—for they say these English are never satisfied unless they marry—"

"Wife! English! Whom are you talking of?"

"Why, the young English signor, to be sure."

"Chut! I thought you spoke of Zicci."

"Oh! Signor Zicci is very rich and very generous; but he wants to be your cavalier, not your husband. I see that,—leave me alone. When you are married, then you will see how amiable Signor Zicci will be. Oh, per fede! but he will be as close to your husband as the yolk to the white; that he will.

"Silence, Gionetta! How wretched I am to have no one else to speak to—to advise me. Oh, beautiful sun!" and the girl pressed her hand to her heart with wild energy, "why do you light every spot but this? Dark, dark! And a little while ago I was so calm, so innocent, so gay. I did not hate you then, Gionetta, hateful as your talk was; I hate you now. Go in; leave me alone—leave me."

"And indeed it is time I should leave you, for the polenta will be spoiled, and you have eaten nothing all day. If you don't eat you will lose your beauty, my darling, and then nobody will care for you. Nobody cares for us when we grow ugly,—I know that; and then you must, like old Gionetta, get some Isabel of your own to spoil. I'll go and see to the polenta."

"Since I have known this man," said the actress, half aloud, "since his dark eyes have fascinated me, I am no longer the same. I long to escape from myself,—to glide with the sunbeam over the hill-tops; to become something that is not of earth. Is it, indeed, that he is a sorcerer, as I have heard? Phantoms float before me at night, and a fluttering like the wing of a bird within my heart seems as if the spirit were terrified, and would break its cage."

While murmuring these incoherent rhapsodies, a step that she did not hear approached the actress, and a light hand touched her arm.

"Isabella! carissima! Isabella!"

She turned, and saw Glyndon. The sight of his fair young face calmed her at once. She did not love him, yet his sight gave her pleasure. She had for him a kind and grateful feeling. Ah, if she had never beheld Zicci!

"Isabel," said the Englishman, drawing her again to the bench from which she had risen, and seating himself beside her, "you know how passionately I love thee. Hitherto thou hast played with my impatience and my ardor, thou hast sometimes smiled, sometimes frowned away my importunities for a reply to my suit; but this day—I know not how it is—I feel a more sustained and settled courage to address thee, and learn the happiest or the worst. I have rivals, I know,—rivals who are more powerful than the poor artist. Are they also more favored?"

Isabel blushed faintly, but her countenance was grave and distressed. Looking down, and marking some hieroglyphical figures in the dust with the point of her slipper, she said, with some hesitation and a vain attempt to be gay, "Signor, whoever wastes his thoughts on an actress must submit to have rivals. It is our unhappy destiny not to be sacred even to ourselves."

"But you have told me, Isabel, that you do not love this destiny, glittering though it seem,—that your heart is not in the vocation which your talents adorn."

"Ah, no!" said the actress, her eyes filling with tears, "it is a miserable lot to be slave to a multitude."

"Fly then with me," said the artist, passionately. "Quit forever the calling that divides that heart I would have all my own. Share my fate now and forever,—my pride, my delight, my ideal! Thou shalt inspire my canvas and my song, thy beauty shall be made at once holy and renowned. In the galleries of princes crowds shall gather round the effigy of a Venus or a saint, and a whisper shall break forth, 'It is Isabel di Pisani!' Ah! Isabel, I adore thee: tell me that I do not worship in vain."

"Thou art good and fair," said Isabel, gazing on her lover as he pressed his cheek nearer to hers, and clasped her hand in his. "But what should I give thee in return?"

"Love, love; only love!"

"A sister's love?"

"Ah, speak not with such cruel coldness!"

"It is all I have for thee. Listen to me, signor. When I look on your face, when I hear your voice, a certain serene and tranquil calm creeps over and lulls thoughts, oh, how feverish, how wild! When thou art gone, the day seems a shade more dark; but the shadow soon flies. I miss thee not, I think not of thee,—no, I love thee not; and I will give myself only where I love."

"But I would teach thee to love me,—fear it not. Nay, such love as thou now describest in our tranquil climates is the love of innocence and youth."

"And it is the innocence he would destroy," said Isabel, rather to herself than to him.

Glyndon drew back, conscience-stricken.

"No, it may not be!" she said, rising, and extricating her hand gently from his grasp. "Leave me, and forget me. You do not understand, you could not comprehend, the nature of her whom you think to love. From my childhood upward, I have felt as if I were marked out for some strange and preternatural doom; as if I were singled from my kind. This feeling (and, oh! at times it is one of delirious and vague delight, at others of the darkest gloom) deepens with me day by day. It is like the shadow of twilight, spreading slowly and solemnly round. My hour approaches; a little while, and it will be night!"

As she spoke, Glyndon listened with visible emotion and perturbation. "Isabel!" he exclaimed, as she ceased, "your words more than ever enchain me to you. As you feel, I feel. I, too, have been ever haunted with a chill and unearthly foreboding. Amidst the crowds of men I have felt alone. In all my pleasures, my toils, my pursuits, a warning voice has murmured in my ear, 'Time has a dark mystery in store for thy manhood.' When you spoke it was as the voice of my own soul."

Isabel gazed upon him in wonder and fear. Her countenance was as white as marble, and those features, so divine in their rare symmetry, might have served the Greek with a study for the Pythoness when, from the mystic cavern and the bubbling spring, she first hears the voice of the inspiring god. Gradually the rigor and tension of that wonderful face relaxed, the color returned, the pulse beat, the heart animated the frame.

"Tell me," she said, turning partially aside, "tell me, have you seen, do you know, a stranger in this city,—one of whom wild stories are afloat?"

"You speak of Zicci. I have seen him; I know him! And you? Ah! he, too, would be my rival,—he, too, would bear thee from me!"

"You err," said Isabel, hastily and with a deep sigh,—"he pleads for you; he informed me of your love; he besought me not—not to reject it."

"Strange being, incomprehensible enigma, why did you name him?"

"Why? Ah! I would have asked whether, when you first saw him, the foreboding, the instinct, of which you spoke came on you more fearfully, more intelligibly than before; whether you felt at once repelled from him, yet attracted towards him; whether you felt [and the actress spoke with hurried animation] that with Him was connected the secret of your life!"

"All this I felt," answered Glyndon, in a trembling voice, "the first time I was in his presence. Though all around me was gay,—music, amidst lamp-lit trees, light converse near, and heaven without a cloud above,—my knees knocked together, my hair bristled, and my blood curdled like ice; since then he has divided my thoughts with thee."

"No more, no more," said Isabel, in a stifled tone; "there must be the hand of Fate in this. I can speak no more to you now; farewell."

She sprang past him into the house and closed the door. Glyndon did not dare to follow her, nor, strange as it may seem, was he so inclined. The thought and recollection of that moonlight hour in the gardens, of the strange address of Zicci, froze up all human passion; Isabel herself, if not forgotten, shrank back like a shadow into the recesses of his breast. He shivered as he stepped into the sunlight, and musingly retraced his steps into the more populous parts of that liveliest of Italian cities.

CHAPTER VIII

It was a small cabinet; the walls were covered with pictures, one of which was worth more than the whole lineage of the owner of the palace. Is not Art a wonderful thing? A Venetian noble might be a fribble or an assassin, a scoundrel, or a dolt, worthless, or worse than worthless; yet he might have sat to Titian, and his portrait may be inestimable,—a few inches of painted canvas a thousand times more valuable than a man with his veins and muscles, brain, will, heart, and intellect!

In this cabinet sat a man of about three and forty,—dark-eyed, sallow, with short, prominent features, a massive conformation of jaw, and thick, sensual, but resolute lips; this man was the Prince di—. His form, middle-sized, but rather inclined to corpulence, was clothed in a loose dressing-robe of rich brocade; on a table before him lay his sword and hat, a mask, dice and dice-box, a portfolio, and an inkstand of silver curiously carved.

"Well, Mascari," said the Prince, looking up towards his parasite, who stood by the embrasure of the deep-set barricaded window, "well, you cannot even guess who this insolent meddler was? A pretty person you to act the part of a Prince's Ruffiano!"

"Am I to be blamed for dulness in not being able to conjecture who had the courage to thwart the projects of the Prince di—. As well blame me for not accounting for miracles."

"I will tell thee who it was, most sapient Mascari."

"Who, your Excellency?"

"Zicci."

"Ah! he has the daring of the devil. But why does your Excellency feel so assured,—does he court the actress?"

"I know not; but there is a tone in that foreigner's voice that I never can mistake,—so clear, and yet so hollow; when I hear it I almost fancy there is such a thing as conscience. However, we must rid ourselves of an impertinent. Mascari, Signor Zicci hath not yet honored our poor house with his presence. He is a distinguished stranger,—we must give a banquet in his honor."

"Ah! and the cypress wine! The cypress is the proper emblem of the grave."

"But this anon. I am superstitious; there are strange stories of his power and foresight,—remember the Sicilian quackery! But meanwhile the Pisani—"

"Your Excellency is infatuated. The actress has bewitched you."

"Mascari," said the Prince, with a haughty smile, "through these veins rolls the blood of the old Visconti,—of those who boasted that no woman ever escaped their lust, and no man their resentment. The crown of my fathers has shrunk into a gewgaw and a toy,—their ambition and their spirit are undecayed. My honor is now enlisted in this pursuit: Isabel must be mine."

"Another ambuscade?" said Mascari, inquiringly.

"Nay, why not enter the house itself? The situation is lonely, and the door is not made of iron."

Before Mascari could reply, the gentleman of the chamber announced the Signor Zicci.

The Prince involuntarily laid his hand on the sword placed on the table; then, with a smile at his own impulse, rose, and met the foreigner at the threshold with all the profuse and respectful courtesy of Italian simulation.

"This is an honor highly prized," said the Prince; "I have long desired the friendship of one so distinguished—"

"And I have come to give you that friendship," replied Zicci, in a sweet but chilling voice. "To no man yet in Naples have I extended this hand: permit it, Prince, to grasp your own."

The Neapolitan bowed over the hand he pressed; but as he touched it, a shiver came over him, and his heart stood still.

Zicci bent on him his dark, smiling eyes, and then seated himself with a familiar air.

"Thus it is signed and sealed,—I mean our friendship, noble Prince. And now I will tell you the object of my visit. I find, your Excellency, that, unconsciously perhaps, we are rivals. Can we not accommodate our pretensions? A girl of no moment, an actress, bah! it is not worth a quarrel. Shall we throw for her? He who casts the lowest shall resign his claim?"

Mascari opened his small eyes to their widest extent; the Prince, no less surprised, but far too well world-read even to show what he felt, laughed aloud.

"And were you, then, the cavalier who spoiled my night's chase and robbed me of my white doe? By Bacchus, it was prettily done."

"You must forgive me, my Prince; I knew not who it was, or my respect would have silenced my gallantry."

"All stratagems fair in love, as in war. Of course you profited by my defeat, and did not content yourself with leaving the little actress at her threshold?"

"She is Diana for me," answered Zicci, lightly; "whoever wins the wreath will not find a flower faded."

"And now you would cast for her,—well; but they tell me you are ever a sure player."

"Let Signor Mascari cast for us."

"Be it so. Mascari, the dice."

Surprised and perplexed, the parasite took up the three dice, deposited them gravely in the box, and rattled them noisily, while Zicci threw himself back carelessly in his chair and said, "I give the first chance to your Excellency."

Mascari interchanged a glance with his patron and threw the numbers were sixteen.

"It is a high throw," said Zicci, calmly; "nevertheless, Signor Mascari, I do not despond."

Mascari gathered up the dice, shook the box, and rolled the contents once more upon the table; the number was the highest that can be thrown,—eighteen.

The Prince darted a glance of fire at his minion, who stood with gaping mouth staring at the dice, and shaking his head in puzzled wonder.

"I have won, you see," said Zicci: "may we be friends still?"

"Signor," said the Prince, obviously struggling with angel and confusion, "the victory is already yours. But, pardon me, you have spoken lightly of this young girl,—will anything tempt you to yield your claim?"

"Ah, do not think so ill of my gallantry."

"Enough," said the Prince, forcing a smile, "I yield. Let me prove that I do not yield ungraciously: will you honor me with your presence at a little feast I propose to give on the royal birthday?"

"It is indeed a happiness to hear one command of yours which I can obey."

Zicci then turned the conversation, talked lightly and gayly and soon afterwards departed.

"Villain," then exclaimed the Prince, grasping Mascari by the collar, "you have betrayed me!"

"I assure your Excellency that the dice were properly arranged,—he should have thrown twelve; but he is the Devil, and that's the end of it."

"There is no time to be lost," said the Prince, quitting hold of his parasite, who quietly resettled his cravat.

"My blood is up! I will win this girl, if I die for it. Who laughed? Mascari, didst thou laugh?"

"I, your Excellency,—I laugh?"

"It sounded behind me," said the Prince, gazing round.

CHAPTER IX

It was the day on which Zicci had told Glyndon that he should ask for his decision in respect to Isabel,—the third day since their last meeting. The Englishman could not come to a resolution. Ambition, hitherto the leading passion of his soul, could not yet be silenced by love, and that love, such as it was, unreturned, beset by suspicions and doubts which vanished in the presence of Isabel, and returned when her bright face shone on his eyes no more, for les absents ont toujours tort. Perhaps had he been quite alone, his feelings of honor, of compassion, of virtue, might have triumphed, and he would have resolved either to fly from Isabel or to offer the love that has no shame. But Merton, cold, cautious, experienced, wary (such a nature has ever power over the imaginative and the impassioned), was at hand to ridicule the impression produced by Zicci, and the notion of delicacy and honor towards an Italian actress. It is true that Merton, who was no profligate, advised him to quit all pursuit of Isabel; but then the advice was precisely of that character which, if it deadens love, stimulates passion. By representing Isabel as one who sought to play a part with him, he excused to Glyndon his own selfishness,—he enlisted the Englishman's vanity and pride on the side of his pursuit. Why should not he beat an adventuress at her own weapons?

Glyndon not only felt indisposed on that day to meet Zicci, but he felt also a strong desire to defeat the mysterious prophecy that the meeting should take place. Into this wish Merton readily entered. The young men agreed to be absent from Naples that day. Early in the morning they mounted their horses and took the road to Baiae. Glyndon left word at his hotel that if Signor Zicci sought him, it was in the neighborhood of the once celebrated watering-place of the ancients that he should be found.

They passed by Isabel's house; but Glyndon resisted the temptation of pausing there, and threading the grotto of Pausilippo, they wound by a circuitous route back into the suburbs of the city, and took the opposite road, which conducts to Portici and Pompeii. It was late at noon when they arrived at the former of these places. Here they halted to dine; for Merton had heard much of the excellence of the macaroni at Portici, and Merton was a bon vivant.

They put up at an inn of very humble pretensions, and dined under an awning. Merton was more than usually gay; he pressed the lacryma upon his friend, and conversed gayly. "Well, my dear friend, we have foiled Signor Zicci in one of his predictions at least. You will have no faith in him hereafter."

"The Ides are come, not gone."

"Tush! if he is a soothsayer, you are not Caesar. It is your vanity that makes you credulous. Thank Heaven, I do not think myself of such importance that the operations of Nature should be changed in order to frighten me."

"But why should the operations of Nature be changed? There may be a deeper philosophy than we dream of,—a philosophy that discovers the secrets of Nature, but does not alter, by penetrating, its courses."

"Ah! you suppose Zicci to be a prophet,—a reader of the future; perhaps an associate of Genii and Spirits!"

"I know not what to conjecture; but I see no reason why he should seek, even if an impostor, to impose on me. An impostor must have some motive for deluding us,—either ambition or avarice. I am neither rich nor powerful; Zicci spends more in a week than I do in a year. Nay, a Neapolitan banker told me that the sums invested by Zicci in his hands, were enough to purchase half the lands of the Neapolitan noblesse."

"Grant this to be true: do you suppose the love to dazzle and mystify is not as strong with some natures as that of gold and power with others? Zicci has a moral ostentation; and the same character that makes him rival kings in expenditure makes him not disdain to be wondered at even by a humble Englishman."

Here the landlord, a little, fat, oily fellow, came up with a fresh bottle of lacryma. He hoped their Excellencies were pleased. He was most touched,—touched to the heart that they liked the macaroni. Were their Excellencies going to Vesuvius? There was a slight eruption; they could not see it where they were, but it was pretty, and would be prettier still after sunset.

"A capital idea," cried Merton. "What say you, Glyndon?"

"I have not yet seen an eruption; I should like it much."

"But is there no danger?" said the prudent Merton.

"Oh! not at all; the mountain is very civil at present. It only plays a little, just to amuse their Excellencies the English."

"Well, order the horses, and bring the bill; we will go before it is dark. Clarence, my friend, nunc est bibendum; but take care of the pede libero, which won't do for walking on lava!"

The bottle was finished, the bill paid, the gentlemen mounted, the landlord bowed, and they bent their way in the cool of the delightful evening towards Resina.

The wine animated Glyndon, whose unequal spirits were at times high and brilliant as those of a school-boy released; and the laughter of the Northern tourists sounded oft and merrily along the melancholy domains of buried cities.

Hesperus had lighted his lamp amidst the rosy skies as they arrived at Resina. Here they quitted their horses and took mules and a guide. As the sky grew darker and more dark, the Mountain Fire burned with an intense lustre. In various streaks and streamlets the fountain of flame rolled down the dark summit, then undiminished by the eruption of 1822, and the Englishmen began to feel increase upon them, as they ascended, that sensation of solemnity and awe which makes the very atmosphere that surrounds the giant of the Plains of the Antique Hades.

It was night when, leaving the mules, they ascended on foot, accompanied by their guide and a peasant, who bore a rude torch. Their guide was a conversable, garrulous fellow, like most of his country and his calling; and Merton, whose chief characteristics were a sociable temper and a hardy commonsense, loved to amuse or to instruct himself on every incidental occasion.

"Ah, Excellency," said the guide, "your countrymen have a strong passion for the volcano. Long life to them; they bring us plenty of money. If our fortunes depended on the Neapolitans, we should starve."

"True, they have no curiosity," said Merton. "Do you remember, Glyndon, the contempt with which that old count said to us, 'You will go to Vesuvius, I suppose. I have never been: why should I go? You have cold, you have hunger, you have fatigue, you have danger, and all for nothing but to see fire, which looks just as well in a brazier as a mountain.' Ha! ha! the old fellow was right."

"But, Excellency," said the guide, "that is not all: some cavaliers think to ascend the mountain without our help. I am sure they deserve to tumble into the crater."

"They must be bold fellows to go alone: you don't often find such?"

"Sometimes among the French, signor. But the other night—I never was so frightened. I had been with an English party, and a lady had left a pocket-book on the mountain where she had been sketching. She offered me a handsome sum to return for it, and bring it to her at Naples; so I went in the evening. I found it sure enough, and was about to return, when I saw a figure that seemed to emerge from the crater itself. The air was so pestiferous that I could not have conceived a human creature could breathe it and live. I was so astounded that I stood as still as a stone, till the figure came over the hot ashes and stood before me face to face. Sancta Maria, what a head!"

"What, hideous?"

"No, so beautiful, but so terrible. It had nothing human in its aspect."

"And what said the salamander?"

"Nothing! It did not even seem to perceive me, though I was as near as I am to you; but its eyes seemed prying into the air. It passed by me quickly, and, walking across a stream of burning lava, soon vanished on the other side of the mountain. I was curious and foolhardy, and resolved to see if I could bear the atmosphere which this visitor had left; but though I did not advance within thirty yards of the spot at which he had first appeared, I was driven back by a vapor that well-nigh stifled me. Cospetto! I have spit blood ever since."

"It must be Zicci," whispered Glyndon.

"I knew you would say so," returned Merton, laughing.

The little party had now arrived nearly at the summit of the mountain; and unspeakably grand was the spectacle on which they gazed. From the crater arose a vapor, intensely dark, that overspread the whole background of the heavens, in the centre whereof rose a flame that assumed a form singularly beautiful. It might have been compared to a crest of gigantic feathers, the diadem of the mountain, high arched, and drooping downward, with the hues delicately shaded off, and the whole shifting and tremulous as the plumage on a warrior's helm. The glare of the flame spread, luminous and crimson, over the dark and rugged ground on which they stood, and drew an innumerable variety of shadows from crag and hollow. An oppressive and sulphureous exhalation served to increase the gloomy and sublime terror of the place. But on turning from the mountain, and towards the distant and unseen ocean, the contrast was wonderfully great: the heavens serene and blue, the stars still and calm as the eyes of Divine Love. It was as if the realms of the opposing principles of Evil and Good were brought in one view before the gaze of man! Glyndon—the enthusiast, the poet, the artist, the dreamer—was enchained and entranced by emotions vague and undefinable, half of delight and half of pain. Leaning on the shoulder of his friend, he gazed around him, and heard, with deepening awe, the rumbling of the earth below, the wheels and voices of the Ministry of Nature in her darkest and most inscrutable recess. Suddenly, as a bomb from a shell, a huge stone was flung hundreds of yards up from the jaws of the crater, and falling with a mighty crash upon the rock below, split into ten thousand fragments, which bounded down the sides of the mountain, sparkling and groaning as they went. One of these, the largest fragment, struck the narrow space of soil between the Englishman and the guide, not three feet from the spot where the former stood. Merton uttered an exclamation of terror, and Glyndon held his breath and shuddered. "Diavolo!" cried the guide; "descend, Excellencies, descend! We have not a moment to lose; follow me close."

So saying, the guide and the peasant fled with as much swiftness as they were able to bring to bear. Merton, ever more prompt and ready than his friend, imitated their example; and Glyndon, more confused than alarmed, followed close. But they had not gone many yards before, with a rushing and sudden blast, came from the crater an enormous volume of vapor. It pursued, it overtook, it overspread them; it swept the light from the heavens. All was abrupt and utter darkness, and through the gloom was heard the shout of the guide, already distant, and lost in an instant amidst the sound of the rushing gust and the groans of the earth beneath. Glyndon paused. He was separated from his friend, from the guide. He was alone with the Darkness and the Terror. The vapor rolled sullenly away; the form of the plumed fire was again dimly visible, and its struggling and perturbed reflection again shed a glow over the horrors of the path. Glyndon recovered himself, and sped onward. Below, he heard the voice of Merton calling on him, though he no longer saw his form. The sound served as a guide. Dizzy and breathless, he bounded forward, when hark! a sullen, slow, rolling sound in his ear! He halted, and turned back to gaze. The fire had overflowed its course; it had opened itself a channel amidst the furrows of the mountain. The stream pursued him fast, fast, and the hot breath of the chasing and preternatural foe came closer and closer upon his cheek. He turned aside; he climbed desperately, with hands and feet, upon a crag that, to the right, broke the scathed and blasted level of the soil. The stream rolled beside and beneath him, and then, taking a sudden wind round the spot on which he stood, interposed its liquid fire—a broad and impassable barrier—between his resting-place and escape. There he stood, cut off from descent, and with no alternative but to retrace his steps towards the crater, and thence seek—without guide or clew—some other pathway.

For a moment his courage left him; he cried in despair, and in that over-strained pitch of voice which is never heard afar off, to the guide, to Merton, to return, to aid him.

No answer came; and the Englishman, thus abandoned solely to his own resources, felt his spirit and energy rise against the danger. He turned back, and ventured as far towards the crater as the noxious exhalation would permit; then, gazing below, carefully and deliberately he chalked out for himself a path, by which he trusted to shun the direction the fire-stream had taken, and trod firmly and quickly over the crumbling and heated strata.

He had proceeded about fifty yards when he halted abruptly: an unspeakable and unaccountable horror, not hitherto felt amidst all his peril, came over him. He shook in every limb; his muscles refused his will; he felt, as it were, palsied and death-stricken. The horror, I say, was unaccountable, for the path seemed clear and safe. The fire, above and behind, burned out clear and far; and beyond, the stars lent him their cheering guidance. No obstacle was visible, no danger seemed at hand. As thus, spell-bound and panic-stricken, he stood chained to the soil—his breast heaving, large drops rolling down his brow, and his eyes starting wildly from their sockets—he saw before him, at some distance, gradually shaping itself more and more distinctly to his gaze, a Colossal Shadow,—a shadow that seemed partially borrowed from the human shape, but immeasurably above the human stature, vague, dark, almost formless and differing—he could not tell where or why—not only from the proportions, but also from the limbs and outline of man.

The glare of the volcano, that seemed to shrink and collapse from this gigantic and appalling apparition, nevertheless threw its light, redly and steadily, upon another shape that stood beside, quiet and motionless; and it was perhaps the contrast of these two things—the Being and the Shadow—that impressed the beholder with the difference between them,—the Man and the Superhuman. It was but for a moment, nay, for the tenth part of a moment, that this sight was permitted to the wanderer. A second eddy of sulphureous vapors from the volcano, yet more rapidly, yet more densely than its predecessor, rolled over the mountain; and either the nature of the exhalation, or the excess of his own dread, was such that Glyndon, after one wild gasp for breath, fell senseless on the earth.

CHAPTER X

Merton and the Italians arrived in safety at the spot where they had left the mules; and not till they had recovered their own alarm and breath did they think of Glyndon. But then, as the minutes passed and he appeared not, Merton—whose heart was as good, at least, as human hearts are in general—grew seriously alarmed. He insisted on returning to search for his friend, and by dint of prodigal promises prevailed at last on the guide to accompany him. The lower part of the mountain lay calm and white in the starlight; and the guide's practised eye could discern all objects on the surface, at a considerable distance. They had not, however, gone very far before they perceived two forms slowly approaching towards them.

As they came near, Merton recognized the form of his friend. "Thank Heaven, he is safe!" he cried, turning to the guide.

"Holy angels befriend us!" said the Italian, trembling; "behold the very being that crossed me last Sabbath night. It is he, but his face is human now!"

"Signor Inglese," said the voice of Zicci as Glyndon, pale, wan, and silent, returned passively the joyous greeting of Merton,—"Signor Inglese, I told your friend we should meet to-night; you see you have not foiled my prediction."

"But how, but where?" stammered Merton, in great confusion and surprise.

"I found your friend stretched on the ground, overpowered by the mephitic exhalation of the crater. I bore him to a purer atmosphere; and as I know the mountain well, I have conducted him safely to you. This is all our history. You see, sir, that were it not for that prophecy which you desired to frustrate, your friend would, ere this time, have been a corpse; one minute more, and the vapor had done its work. Adieu! good night and pleasant dreams."

"But, my preserver, you will not leave us," said Glyndon, anxiously, and speaking for the first time. "Will you not return with us?"

Zicci paused, and drew Glyndon aside. "Young man," said he, gravely, "it is necessary that we should again meet to-night. It is necessary that you should, ere the first hour of morning, decide on your fate. Will you marry Isabel di Pisani, or lose her forever? Consult not your friend; he is sensible and wise, but not now is his wisdom needed. There are times in life when from the imagination, and not the reason, should wisdom come,—this for you is one of them. I ask not your answer now. Collect your thoughts, recover your jaded and scattered spirits. It wants two hours of midnight: at midnight I will be with you!"

"Incomprehensible being," replied the Englishman, "I would leave the life you have preserved in your own hands. But since I have known you, my whole nature has changed. A fiercer desire than that of love burns in my veins,—the desire, not to resemble, but to surpass my kind; the desire to penetrate and to share the secret of your own existence; the desire of a preternatural knowledge and unearthly power. Instruct me, school me, make me thine; and I surrender to thee at once, and without a murmur, the woman that, till I saw thee, I would have defied a world to obtain."

"I ask not the sacrifice, Glyndon," replied Zicci, coldly, yet mildly, "yet—shall I own it to thee?—I am touched by the devotion I have inspired. I sicken for human companionship, sympathy, and friendship; yet I dread to share them, for bold must be the man who can partake my existence and enjoy my confidence. Once more I say to thee, in compassion and in warning, the choice of life is in thy hands,—to-morrow it will be too late. On the one hand, Isabel, a tranquil home, a happy and serene life; on the other hand all is darkness, darkness that even this eye cannot penetrate."

"But thou hast told me that if I wed Isabel I must be contented to be obscure; and if I refuse, that knowledge and power may be mine."

"Vain man! knowledge and power are not happiness."

"But they are better than happiness. Say, if I marry Isabel, wilt thou be my master, my guide? Say this, and I am resolved."

"Never! It is only the lonely at heart, the restless, the desperate, that may be my pupils."

"Then I renounce her! I renounce love, I renounce happiness. Welcome solitude, welcome despair, if they are the entrances to thy dark and sublime secret."

"I will not take thy answer now; at midnight thou shalt give it in one word,—ay, or no! Farewell till then!"

The mystic waved his hand, and descending rapidly, was seen no more.

Glyndon rejoined his impatient and wondering friend; but Merton, gazing on his face, saw that a great change had passed there. The flexile and dubious expression of youth was forever gone; the features were locked, rigid, and stern; and so faded was the natural bloom that an hour seemed to have done the work of years.

CHAPTER, XI

On returning from Vesuvius or Pompeii you enter Naples through its most animated, its most Neapolitan quarter, through that quarter in which Modern life most closely resembles the Ancient, and in which, when, on a fair day, the thoroughfare swarms alike with Indolence and Trade, you are impressed at once with the recollection of that restless, lively race from which the population of Naples derives its origin; so that in one day you may see at Pompeii the habitations of a remote age, and on the Mole at Naples you may imagine you behold the very beings with which those habitations had been peopled. The language of words is dead, but the language of gestures remains little impaired. A fisherman,—peasant, of Naples will explain to you the motions, the attitudes, the gestures of the figures painted on the antique vases better than the most learned antiquary of Gottingen or Leipsic.

But now, as the Englishmen rode slowly through the deserted streets, lighted but by the lamps of heaven, all the gayety of the day was hushed and breathless. Here and there, stretched under a portico or a dingy booth, were sleeping groups of houseless lazzaroni,—a tribe now happily merging this indolent individuality amidst an energetic and active population.

The Englishmen rode on in silence, for Glyndon neither appeared to heed or hear the questions and comments of Merton, and Merton himself was almost as weary as the jaded animal he bestrode.

Suddenly the silence of earth and ocean was broken by the sound of a distant clock, that proclaimed the last hour of night. Glyndon started from his revery, and looked anxiously around. As the final stroke died, the noise of hoofs rang on the broad stones of the pavement, and from a narrow street to the right emerged the form of a solitary horseman. He neared the Englishmen, and Glyndon recognized the features and mien of Zicci.

"What! do we meet again, signor?" said Merton, in a vexed but drowsy tone.

"Your friend and I have business together," replied Zicci, as he wheeled his powerful and fiery steed to the side of Glyndon; "but it will be soon transacted. Perhaps you, sir, will ride on to your hotel."

"Alone?"

"There is no danger," returned Zicci, with a slight expression of disdain in his voice.

"None to me, but to Glyndon?"

"Danger from me? Ah! perhaps you are right."

"Go on, my dear Merton," said Glyndon. "I will join you before you reach the hotel."

Merton nodded, whistled, and pushed his horse into a kind of amble.

"Now your answer,—quick."

"I have decided: the love of Isabel has vanished from my heart. The pursuit is over."

"You have decided?"

"I have."

"Adieu! join your friend."

Zicci gave the rein to his horse; it sprang forward with a bound; the sparks flew from its hoofs, and horse and rider disappeared amidst the shadows of the street whence they had emerged.

Merton was surprised to see his friend by his side, a minute after they had parted.

"What business can you have with Zicci? Will you not confide in me?"

"Merton, do not ask me to-night; I am in a dream."

"I do not wonder at it, for even I am in a sleep. Let us push on."

In the retirement of his chamber, Glyndon sought to recollect his thoughts. He sat down on the foot of his bed and pressed his hands tightly to his throbbing temples. The events of the last few hours, the apparition of the gigantic and shadowy Companion of the Mystic amidst the fires and clouds of Vesuvius, the strange encounter with Zicci himself on a spot in which he could never have calculated on finding Glyndon, filled his mind with emotions, in which terror and awe the least prevailed. A fire, the train of which had long been laid, was lighted at his heart,—the asbestos fire that, once lit, is never to be quenched. All his early aspiration, his young ambition, his longings for the laurel, were mingled in one passionate yearning to overpass the bounds of the common knowledge of man, and reach that solemn spot, between two worlds, on which the mysterious stranger appeared to have fixed his home.

Far from recalling with renewed affright the remembrance of the apparition that had so appalled him, the recollection only served to kindle and concentrate his curiosity into a burning focus. He had said aright,—love had vanished from his heart; there was no longer a serene space amidst its disordered elements for human affection to move and breathe. The enthusiast was rapt from this earth; and he would have surrendered all that beauty ever promised, that mortal hope ever whispered, for one hour with Zicci beyond the portals of the visible world.

He rose, oppressed and fevered with the new thoughts that raged within him, and threw open his casement for air. The ocean lay suffused in the starry light, and the stillness of the heavens never more eloquently preached the morality of repose to the madness of earthly passions. But such was Glyndon's mood that their very hush only served to deepen the wild desires that preyed upon his soul. And the solemn stars, that are mysteries in themselves, seemed by a kindred sympathy to agitate the wings of the spirit no longer contented with its cage. As he gazed, a star shot from its brethren and vanished from the depth of space!

CHAPTER XII

The sleep of Glyndon that night was unusually profound, and the sun streamed full upon his eyes as he opened them to the day. He rose refreshed, and with a strange sentiment of calmness, that seemed more the result of resolution than exhaustion. The incidents and emotions of the past night had settled into distinct and clear impressions. He thought of them but slightly,—he thought rather of the future. He was as one of the Initiated in the old Egyptian Mysteries, who have crossed the Gate only to look more ardently for the Penetralia.

He dressed himself, and was relieved to find that Merton had joined a party of his countrymen on an excursion to Ischia. He spent the heat of noon in thoughtful solitude, and gradually the image of Isabel returned to his heart. It was a holy—for it was a human—image; he had resigned her, and he repented. The light of day served, if not to dissipate, at least to sober, the turbulence and fervor of the preceding night. But was it indeed too late to retract his resolve? "Too late!" terrible words! Of what do we not repent, when the Ghost of the Deed returns to us to say, "Thou hast no recall?"

He started impatiently from his seat, seized his hat and sword, and strode with rapid steps to the humble abode of the actress.

The distance was considerable, and the air oppressive. Glyndon arrived at the door breathless and heated he knocked, no answer came; he lifted the latch and entered. No sound, no sight of life, met his ear and eye. In the front chamber, on a table, lay the guitar of the actress and some manuscript parts in plays. He paused, and summoning courage, tapped at the door which seemed to lead into the inner apartment. The door was ajar; and hearing no sound within, he pushed it open. It was the sleeping chamber of the young actress,—that holiest ground to a lover. And well did the place become the presiding deity: none of the tawdry finery of the Profession was visible on the one hand, none of the slovenly disorder common to the humbler classes of the South on the other. All was pure and simple; even the ornaments were those of an innocent refinement,—a few books placed carefully on shelves, a few half-faded flowers in an earthen vase which was modelled and painted in the Etruscan fashion. The sunlight streamed over the snowy draperies of the bed, and a few articles of clothing, neatly folded, on the chair beside it. Isabel was not there; and Glyndon, as he gazed around, observed that the casement which opened to the ground was wrenched and broken, and several fragments of the shattered glass lay below. The light flashed at once upon Glyndon's mind,—the ravisher had borne away his prize. The ominous words of Zicci were fulfilled: it was too late! Wretch that he was, perhaps he might have saved her! But the nurse,—was she gone also? He made the house resound with the name of Gionetta, but there was not even an echo to reply. He resolved to repair at once to the abode of Zicci. On arriving at the palace of the Corsican, he was informed that the signor was gone to the banquet of the Prince di—, and would not return until late. He turned in dismay from the door, and perceived the heavy carriage of the Count Cetoxa rolling along the narrow street. Cetoxa recognized him and stopped the carriage.

"Ah my dear Signor Glyndon," said he, leaning out of the window, "and how goes your health? You heard the news?"

"What news?" asked Glyndon, mechanically.

"Why, the beautiful actress,—the wonder of Naples! I always thought she would have good luck."

"Well, well, what of her?"

"The Prince di—has taken a prodigious fancy to her, and has carried her to his own palace. The Court is a little scandalized."

"The villain! by force?"

"Force! Ha! ha! my dear signor, what need of force to persuade an actress to accept the splendid protection of one of the wealthiest noblemen in Italy? Oh, no! you may be sure she went willingly enough. I only just heard the news: the prince himself proclaimed his triumph this morning, and the accommodating Mascari has been permitted to circulate it. I hope the connection will not last long, or we shall lose our best singer. Addio!"

Glyndon stood mute and motionless. He knew not what to think, to believe, or how to act. Even Merton was not at hand to advise him. His conscience smote him bitterly; and half in despair, half in the courageous wrath of jealousy, he resolved to repair to the palace of the prince himself, and demand his captive in the face of his assembled guests.

CHAPTER XIII

We must go back to the preceding night. The actress and her nurse had returned from the theatre; and Isabel, fatigued and exhausted, had thrown herself on a sofa, while Gionetta busied herself with the long tresses which, released from the fillet that bound them, half concealed the form of the actress, like a veil of threads of gold; and while she smoothed the luxuriant locks, the old nurse ran gossiping on about the little events of the night,—the scandal and politics of the scenes and the tire-room.

The clock sounded the hour of midnight, and still Isabel detained the nurse; for a vague and foreboding fear, she could not account for, made her seek to protract the time of solitude and rest.

At length Gionetta's voice was swallowed up in successive yawns. She took her lamp and departed to her own room, which was placed in the upper story of the house. Isabel was alone. The half-hour after midnight sounded dull and distant, all was still, and she was about to enter her sleeping-room, when she heard the hoofs of a horse at full speed. The sound ceased; there was a knock at the door. Her heart beat violently; but fear gave way to another sentiment when she heard a voice, too well known, calling on her name. She went to the door.

"Open, Isabel,—it is Zicci," said the voice again.

And why did the actress feel fear no more, and why did that virgin hand unbar the door to admit, without a scruple or, a doubt, at that late hour, the visit of the fairest cavalier of Naples? I know not; but Zicci had become her destiny, and she obeyed the voice of her preserver as if it were the command of Fate.

Zicci entered with a light and hasty step. His horseman's cloak fitted tightly to his noble form, and the raven plumes of his broad hat threw a gloomy shade over his commanding features.

The girl followed him into the room, trembling and blushing deeply, and stood before him with the lamp she held shining upward on her cheek, and the long hair that fell like a shower of light over the bare shoulders and heaving bust.

"Isabel," said Zicci, in a voice that spoke deep emotion, "I am by thy side once more to save thee. Not a moment is to be lost. Thou must fly with me, or remain the victim of the Prince di—. I would have made the charge I now undertake another's,—thou knowest I would, thou knowest it; but he is not worthy of thee, the cold Englishman! I throw myself at thy feet; have trust in me, and fly."

He grasped her hand passionately as he dropped on his knee, and looked up into her face with his bright, beseeching eyes.

"Fly with thee!" said Isabel, tenderly.

"Thou knowest the penalty,—name, fame, honor, all will be sacrificed if thou dost not."

"Then, then," said the wild girl, falteringly, and turning aside her face, "then I am not indifferent to thee. Thou wouldest not give me to another; thou lovest me?"

Zicci was silent; but his breast heaved, his cheeks flushed, his eyes darted dark but impassioned fire.

"Speak!" exclaimed Isabel, in jealous suspicion of his silence. "Speak, if thou lovest me."

"I dare not tell thee so; I will not yet say I love thee."

"Then what matter my fate?" said Isabel, turning pale and shrinking from his side. "Leave me; I fear no danger. My life, and therefore my honor, is in mine own hands."

"Be not so mad!" said Zicci. "Hark! do you hear the neigh of my steed? It is an alarm that warns us of the approaching peril. Haste, or you are lost."

"Why do you care for me?" said the girl, bitterly. "Thou hast read my heart; thou knowest that I would fly with thee to the end of the world, if I were but sure of thy love; that all sacrifice of womanhood's repute were sweet to me, if regarded as the proof and seal of affection. But to be bound beneath the weight of a cold obligation; to be the beggar on the eyes of Indifference; to throw myself on one who loves me not,—that were indeed the vilest sin of my sex. Ah! Zicci, rather let me die."

She had thrown back her clustering hair from her face as she spoke; and as she now stood, with her arms drooping mournfully, and her hands clasped together with the proud bitterness of her wayward spirit, giving new zest and charm to her singular beauty, it was impossible to conceive a sight more irresistible to the senses and the heart.

"Tempt me not to thine own danger, perhaps destruction," exclaimed Zicci, in faltering accents; "thou canst not dream of what thou wouldest demand. Come," and, advancing, he wound his arm round her waist, "come, Isabel! Believe at least in my friendship, my protection—"

"And not thy love," said the Italian, turning on him her hurried and reproachful eyes. Those eyes met his, and he could not withdraw from the charm of their gaze. He felt her heart throbbing beneath his own; her breath came warm upon his cheek. He trembled,—he, the lofty, the mysterious Zicci,—who seemed to stand aloof from his race. With a deep and burning sigh he murmured, "Isabel, I love thee!" That beautiful face, bathed in blushes, drooped upon his bosom; and as he bent down, his lips sought the rosy mouth,—a long and burning kiss. Danger, life, the world were forgotten! Suddenly Zicci tore himself from her.

"Oh! what have I said? It is gone,—my power to preserve thee, to guard thee, to foresee the storm in thy skies, is gone forever. No matter! Haste, haste; and may love supply the loss of prophecy and power!"

Isabel hesitated no more. She threw her mantle over her shoulders and gathered up her dishevelled hair; a moment, and she was prepared,—when a sudden crash was heard in the inner room.

"Too late!—fool that I was—too late!" cried Zicci, in a sharp tone of agony as he hurried to the outer door. He opened it, only to be borne back by the press of armed men.

Behind, before, escape was cut off. The room literally swarmed with the followers of the ravisher, masked, mailed, armed to the teeth.

Isabel was already in the grasp of two of the myrmidons; her shriek smote the ear of Zicci. He sprang forward, and Isabel heard his wild cry in a foreign tongue,—the gleam, the clash of swords. She lost her senses; and when she recovered, she found herself gagged, and in a carriage that was driven rapidly, by the side of a masked and motionless figure. The carriage stopped at the portals of a gloomy mansion. The gates opened noiselessly, a broad flight of steps, brilliantly illumined, was before her,—she was in the palace of the Prince di—.

CHAPTER XIV

The young actress was led to and left alone in a chamber adorned with all the luxurious and half-Eastern taste that at one time characterized the palaces of the great seigneurs of Italy. Her first thought was for Zicci,—was he yet living? Had he escaped unscathed the blades of the foe,—her new treasure, the new light of her life, her lord, at last her lover?

She had short time for reflection. She heard steps approaching the chamber; she drew back. She placed her hand on the dagger that at all hours she wore concealed in her bosom. Living or dead, she would be faithful still to Zicci There was a new motive to the preservation of honor. The door opened, and the Prince entered, in a dress that sparkled with jewels.

"Fair and cruel one," said he, advancing, with a half-sneer upon his lip, "thou wilt not too harshly blame the violence of love." He attempted to take her hand as he spoke.

"Nay," said he, as she recoiled, "reflect that thou art now in the power of one that never faltered in the pursuit of an object less dear to him than thou art. Thy lover, presumptuous though he be, is not by to save thee. Mine thou art; but instead of thy master, suffer me to be thy slave."

"My lord," said Isabel, with a stern gravity which perhaps the Stage had conspired with Nature, to bestow upon her, "your boast is in vain. Your power,—I am not in your power! Life and death are in my own hands. I will not defy, but I do not fear you. I feel—and in some feelings," added Isabel, with a solemnity almost thrilling, "there is all the strength and all the divinity of knowledge—I feel that I am safe even here; but you, you, Prince di—, have brought danger to your home and hearth!"

The Neapolitan seemed startled by an earnestness and a boldness he was but little prepared for. He was not, however, a man easily intimidated or deterred from any purpose he had formed; and approaching Isabel, he was about to reply with much warmth, real or affected, when a knock was heard at the door of the chamber. The sound was repeated, and the Prince, chafed at the interruption, opened the door and demanded impatiently who had ventured to disobey his orders and invade his leisure. Mascari presented himself, pale and agitated. "My lord," said he, in a whisper, "pardon me, but a stranger is below who insists on seeing you; and from some words he let fall, I judged it advisable even to infringe your commands."

"A stranger, and at this hour! What business can he pretend? Why was he even admitted?"

"He asserts that your life is in imminent danger. The source whence it proceeds he will relate to your Excellency alone."

The Prince frowned, but his color changed. He mused a moment, and then, re-entering the chamber and advancing towards Isabel, he said,—

"Believe me, fair creature, I have no wish to take advantage of my power. I would fain trust alone to the gentler authorities of affection. Hold yourself queen within these walls more absolutely than you have ever enacted that part on the stage. To-night, farewell! May your sleep becalm, and your dreams propitious to my hopes!"

With these words he retired, and in a few moments Isabel was surrounded by officious attendants, whom she at length, with some difficulty, dismissed; and refusing to retire to rest, she spent the night in examining the chamber, which she found was secured, and in thoughts of Zicci, in whose power she felt an almost preternatural confidence.

Meanwhile the Prince descended the stairs, and sought the room into which the stranger had been shown.

He found him wrapped from head to foot in a long robe,—half gown, half mantle,—such as was sometimes worn by ecclesiastics. The face of this stranger was remarkable; so sunburnt and swarthy were his hues that he must, apparently, have derived his origin amongst the races of the farthest East.

His—forehead was lofty, and his eyes so penetrating, yet so calm, in their gaze that the Prince shrank from them as we shrink from a questioner who is drawing forth the guiltiest secrets of our hearts.

"What would you with me?" asked the Prince, motioning his visitor to a seat.

"Prince di—," said the stranger, in a voice deep and sweet, but foreign in its accent, "son of the most energetic and masculine race that ever applied godlike genius to the service of the Human Will, with its winding wickedness and its stubborn grandeur; descendant of the great Visconti, in whose chronicles lies the History of Italy in her palmy day, and in whose rise was the development of the mightiest intellect ripened by the most relentless ambition,—I come to gaze upon the last star in a darkening firmament. By this hour to-morrow space shall know it not. Man, thy days are cumbered!"

"What means this jargon?" said the Prince, in visible astonishment and secret awe. "Comest thou to menace me in my own halls, or wouldest thou warn me of a danger? Art thou some itinerant mountebank, or some unguessed of friend? Speak out, and plainly. What danger threatens me?"

"Zicci!" replied the stranger.

"Ha! ha!" said the Prince, laughing scornfully; "I half suspected thee from the first. Thou art, then, the accomplice or the tool of that most dexterous, but, at present, defeated charlatan. And I suppose thou wilt tell me that if I were to release a certain captive I have made, the danger would vanish and the hand of the dial would be put back?"

"Judge of me as thou wilt, Prince di—. I confess my knowledge of Zicci,—a knowledge shared but by a few, who—But this touches thee not. I would save, therefore I warn thee. Dost thou ask me why? I will tell thee. Canst thou remember to have heard wild tales of thy grandsire,—of his desire for a knowledge that passes that of the schools and cloisters; of a strange man from the East, who was his familiar and master in lore, against which the Vatican has from age to age launched its mimic thunder? Dost thou call to mind the fortunes of thy ancestor,—how he succeeded in youth to little but a name; how, after a career wild and dissolute as thine, he disappeared from Milan, a pauper and a self-exile; how, after years spent none knew in what climes or in what pursuits, he again revisited the city where his progenitors had reigned; how with him came this wise man of the East, the mystic Mejnour; how they who beheld him, beheld with amaze and fear that time had ploughed no furrow on his brow,—that youth seemed fixed as by a spell upon his face and form? Dost thou know that from that hour his fortunes rose? Kinsmen the most remote died, estate upon estate fell into the hands of the ruined noble. He allied himself with the royalty of Austria, he became the guide of princes, the first magnate of Italy. He founded anew the house of which thou art the last lineal upholder, and transferred its splendor from Milan to the Sicilian realms. Visions of high ambition were then present with him nightly and daily. Had he lived, Italy would have known a new dynasty, and the Visconti would have reigned over Magna Graecia. He was a man such as the world rarely sees; he was worthy to be of us, worthy to be the pupil of Mejnour,—whom you now see before you."

The Prince, who had listened with deep and breathless attention to the words of his singular guest, started from his seat at his last words. "Impostor!" he cried, "can you dare thus to play with my credulity? Sixty years have passed since my grandsire died; and you, a man younger apparently than myself, have the assurance to pretend to have been his contemporary! But you have imperfectly learned your tale. You know not, it seems, that my grandsire—wise and illustrious, indeed, in all save his faith in a charlatan—was found dead in his bed in the very hour when his colossal plans were ripe for execution, and that Mejnour was guilty of his murder?"

"Alas!" answered the stranger, in a voice of great sadness, "had he but listened to Mejnour, had he delayed the last and most perilous ordeal of daring wisdom until the requisite training and initiation had been completed, your ancestor would have stood with me upon an eminence which the waters of Death itself wash everlastingly, but cannot overflow. Your grandsire resisted my fervent prayers, disobeyed my most absolute commands, and in the sublime rashness of a soul that panted for the last secrets, perished,—the victim of his own frenzy."

"He was poisoned, and Mejnour fled."

"Mejnour fled not," answered the stranger, quickly and proudly.

"Mejnour could not fly from danger, for to him danger is a thing long left behind. It was the day before the duke took the fatal draught which he believed was to confer on the mortal the immortal boon that, finding my power over him was gone, I abandoned him to his doom.

"On the night on which your grandsire breathed his last, I was standing alone at moonlight on the ruins of Persepolis,—for my wanderings, space hath no obstacle. But a truce with this: I loved your grandsire; I would save the last of his race. Oppose not thyself to Zicci. Oppose not thyself to thine evil passions. Draw back from the precipice while there is yet time. In thy front and in thine eyes I detect some of that diviner glory which belonged to thy race. Thou hast in thee some germs of their hereditary genius, but they are choked up by worse than thy hereditary vices. Recollect, by genius thy house rose,—by vice it ever failed to perpetuate its power. In the laws which regulate the Universe it is decreed that nothing wicked can long endure. Be wise, and let history warn thee. Thou standest on the verge of two worlds,—the Past and the Future; and voices from either shriek omen in thy ear. I have done. I bid thee farewell."

"Not so; thou shalt not quit these walls. I will make experiment of thy boasted power. What ho there! ho!" The Prince shouted; the room was filled with his minions. "Seize that man!" he cried, pointing to the spot which had been filled by the form of Mejnour. To his inconceivable amaze and horror, the spot was vacant. The mysterious stranger had vanished like a dream.

CHAPTER XV

It was the first faint and gradual break of the summer dawn; and two men stood in a balcony overhanging a garden fragrant with the scents of the awakening flowers. The stars had not left the sky, the birds were yet silent on the boughs; all was still, hushed, and tranquil. But how different the tranquillity of reviving day from the solemn repose of night.

In the music of silence there are a thousand variations. These men, who alone seemed awake in Naples, were Zicci and the mysterious stranger, who had but an hour or two ago startled the Prince di—in his voluptuous palace.

"No," said the latter, "hadst thou delayed the acceptance of the Arch Gift until thou hadst attained to the years and passed through all the desolate bereavements that chilled and scared myself ere my researches had made it mine, thou wouldest have escaped the curse of which thou complainest now. Thou wouldest not have mourned over the brevity of human affection as compared to the duration of thine own existence, for thou wouldest have survived the very desire and dream of the love of woman. Brightest, and but for that error perhaps the loftiest, of the secret and solemn race that fills up the interval in creation between mankind and the demons, age after age wilt thou rue the splendid folly which made thee ask to carry the beauty and the passions of youth into the dreary grandeur of earthly immortality."

"I do not repent, nor shall I," answered Zicci, coldly. "The transport and the sorrow, so wildly blended, which diversify my doom, are better than the calm and bloodless tenor of thy solitary way. Thou, who lovest nothing, hatest nothing,—feelest nothing, and walkest the world with the noiseless and joyless footsteps of a dream!"

"You mistake," replied he who had owned the name of Mejnour; "though I care not for love, and am dead to every passion that agitates the sons of clay, I am not dead to their more serene enjoyments. I have still left to me the sublime pleasures of wisdom and of friendship. I carry down the Stream of the countless years, not the turbulent desires of youth, but the calm and spiritual delights of age. Wisely and deliberately I abandoned youth forever when I separated my lot from men. Let us not envy or reproach each other. I would have saved this Neapolitan, Zicci (since so it now pleases thee to be called), partly because his grandsire was but divided by the last airy barrier from our own brotherhood, partly because I know that in the man himself lurk the elements of ancestral courage and power, which in earlier life would have fitted him for one of us. Earth holds but few to whom nature has given the qualities that can bear the ordeal! But time and excess, that have thickened the grosser senses, have blunted the imagination. I relinquish him to his doom."

"And still then, Mejnour, you cherish the desire to increase our scanty and scattered host by new converts and allies; Surely, surely, thy experience might have taught thee that scarcely once in a thousand years is born the being who can pass through the horrible gates that lead into the worlds without. Is not thy path already strewed with thy victims? Do not their ghastly faces of agony and fear,—the blood-stained suicide, the raving maniac,—rise before thee and warn what is yet left to thee of human sympathy from thy insane ambition?"

"Nay," answered Mejnour, "have I not had success to counterbalance failure? And can I forego this lofty and august hope, worthy alone of our high condition,—the hope to form a mighty and numerous race, with a force and power sufficient to permit them to acknowledge to mankind their majestic conquests and dominion; to become the true lords of this planet, invaders perchance of others, masters of the inimical and malignant tribes by which at this moment we are surrounded,—a race that may proceed, in their deathless destinies, from stage to stage of celestial glory, and rank at last among the nearest ministrants and agents gathered round the Throne of Thrones? What matter a thousand victims for one convert to our band? And you, Zicci," continued Mejnour, after a pause, "you, even you, should this affection for a mortal beauty that you have dared, despite yourself, to cherish, be more than a passing fancy; should it, once admitted into your inmost nature, partake of its bright and enduring essence,—even you may brave all things to raise the beloved one into your equal. Nay, interrupt me not. Can you see sickness menace her, danger hover around, years creep on, the eyes grow dim, the beauty fade, while the heart, youthful still, clings and fastens round your own,—can you see this, and know it is yours to—"

"Cease," cried Zicci, fiercely. "What is all other fate as compared to the death of terror? What! when the coldest sage, the most heated enthusiast, the hardiest warrior, with his nerves of iron, have been found dead in their beds, with straining eyeballs and horrent hair, at the first step of the Dread Progress, thinkest thou that this weak woman—from whose cheek a sound at the window, the screech of the night-owl, the sight of a drop of blood on a man's sword, would start the color—could brave one glance of—Away! the very thought of such sights for her makes even myself a coward!"

"When you told her you loved her, when you clasped her to your breast, you renounced all power to prophesy her future lot or protect her from harm. Henceforth to her you are human, and human only. How know you, then, to what you may be tempted? How know you what her curiosity may learn and her courage brave? But enough of this,—you are bent on your pursuit?"

"The fiat has gone forth."

"And to-morrow?"

"To-morrow at this hour our bark will be bounding over yonder ocean, and the weight of ages will have fallen from my heart! Fool, thou hast given up thy youth!"

CHAPTER XVI

The Prince di—was not a man whom Naples could suppose to be addicted to superstitious fancies, neither was the age one in which the belief of sorcery was prevalent. Still, in the South of Italy there was then, and there still lingers, a certain spirit of credulity, which may, ever and anon, be visible amidst the boldest dogmas of their philosophers and sceptics. In his childhood the Prince had learned strange tales of the ambition, the genius, and the career of his grandsire; and secretly, perhaps influenced by ancestral example, in earlier youth he himself had followed alchemy, not only through her legitimate course, but her antiquated and erratic windings. I have, indeed, been shown in Naples a little volume blazoned with the arms of the Visconti, and ascribed to the nobleman I refer to, which treats of alchemy in a spirit half mocking and half reverential.

Pleasure soon distracted him from such speculations, and his talents, which were unquestionably great, were wholly perverted to extravagant intrigues or to the embellishment of a gorgeous ostentation with something of classic grace. His immense wealth, his imperious pride, his unscrupulous and daring character, made him an object of no inconsiderable fear to a feeble and timid court; and the ministers of the indolent government willingly connived at excesses—, which allured him at least from ambition. The strange visit and yet more strange departure of Mejnour filled the breast of the Neapolitan with awe and wonder, against which all the haughty arrogance and learned scepticism of his maturer manhood combated in vain. The apparition of—Mejnour served, indeed, to invest Zicci with a character in which the Prince had not hitherto regarded him. He felt a strange alarm at the rival he had braved, at the foe he had provoked. His night was sleepless, and the next morning he came to the resolution of leaving Isabel in peace until after the banquet of that day, to which he had invited Zicci. He felt as if the death of the mysterious Corsican were necessary for the preservation of his own life; and if at an earlier period of their rivalry he had determined on the fate of Zicci, the warnings of—Mejnour only served to confirm his resolve.

"We will try if his magic can invent an antidote to the bane," said he, half aloud and with a gloomy smile, as he summoned Mascari to his presence. The poison which the Prince, with his own hands, mixed into the wine intended for his guest was compounded from materials the secret of which had been one of the proudest heir-looms of that able and evil race which gave to Italy her wisest and fellest tyrants. Its operation was quick, not sudden; it produced no pain, it left on the form no grim convulsion, on the skin no purpling spot, to arouse suspicion; you might have cut and carved every membrane and fibre of the corpse, but the sharpest eyes of the leech would not have detected the presence of the subtle life-queller. For twelve hours the victim felt nothing, save a joyous and elated exhilaration of the blood; a delicious languor followed,—the sure forerunner of apoplexy. No lancet then could save! Apoplexy had run much in the families of the enemies of the Visconti!

The hour of the feast arrived, the guests assembled. There were the flower of the Neapolitan seigneurie,—the descendants of the Norman, the Teuton, the Goth; for Naples had then a nobility, but derived it from the North, which has indeed been the Nutrix Leonum, the nurse of the lion-hearted chivalry of the world.

Last of the guests came Zicci, and the crowd gave way as the dazzling foreigner moved along to the lord of the palace. The Prince greeted him with a meaning smile, to which Zicci answered by a whisper: "He who plays with loaded dice does not always win."

The Prince bit his lip; and Zicci, passing on, seemed deep in conversation with the fawning Mascari.

"Who is the Prince's heir?" asked the Corsican.

"A distant relation on the mother's side; with his Excellency dies the male line."

"Is the heir present at our host's banquet?"

"No; they are not friends."

"No matter; he will be here to-morrow!"

Mascari stared in surprise; but the signal for the banquet was given, and the guests were marshalled to the board. As was the custom, the feast took place at midday. It was a long oval hall, the whole of one side opening by a marble colonnade upon a court or garden, in which the eye rested gratefully upon cool fountains and statues of whitest marble, half sheltered by orange-trees. Every art that luxury could invent to give freshness and coolness to the languid and breezeless heat of the day without (a day on which the breath of the sirocco was abroad) had been called into existence. Artificial currents of air through invisible tubes, silken blinds waving to and fro as if to cheat the senses into the belief of an April wind, and miniature jets d'eau in each corner of the apartment gave to the Italians the same sense of exhilaration and comfort (if I may use the word) which the well-drawn curtains and the blazing hearth afford to the children of colder climes.

The conversation was somewhat more lively and intellectual than is common among the languid pleasure-hunters of the South; for the Prince, himself accomplished, sought his acquaintance not only amongst the beaux esprits of his own country, but amongst the gay foreigners who adorned and relieved the monotony of the Neapolitan circles. There were present two or three of the brilliant

Frenchmen of the old regime, and their peculiar turn of thought and wit was well calculated for the meridian of a society that made the dolce far niente at once its philosophy and its faith. The Prince, however, was more silent than usual, and when he sought to rouse himself, his spirits were forced and exaggerated. To the manners of his host, those of Zicci afforded a striking contrast. The bearing of this singular person was at all times characterized by a calm and polished ease which was attributed by the courtiers to the long habit of society. He could scarcely be called gay, yet few persons more tended to animate the general spirits of a convivial circle. He seemed, by a kind of intuition, to elicit from each companion the qualities in which he most excelled; and a certain tone of latent mockery that characterized his remarks upon the topics on which the conversation fell, seemed to men who took nothing in earnest to be the language both of wit and wisdom. To the Frenchmen in particular there was something startling in his intimate knowledge of the minutest events in their own capital and country, and his profound penetration (evinced but in epigrams and sarcasms) into the eminent characters who were then playing a part upon the great stage of Continental intrigue. It was while this conversation grew animated, and the feast was at its height, that Glyndon (who, as the reader will recollect, had resolved, on learning from Cetoxa the capture of the actress, to seek the Prince himself) arrived at the palace. The porter, perceiving by his dress that he was not one of the invited guests, told him that his Excellency was engaged, and on no account could be disturbed; and Glyndon then, for the first time, became aware of how strange and embarrassing was the duty he had taken on himself. To force an entrance into the banquet-hall of a great and powerful noble surrounded by the rank of Naples, and to arraign him for what to his boon companions would appear but an act of gallantry, was an exploit that could not fail to be at once ludicrous and impotent. He mused a moment; and remembering that Zicci was among the guests, determined to apply himself to the Corsican. He therefore, slipping a few crowns into the porter's hand, said that he was commissioned to seek the Signor Zicci upon an errand of life and death, and easily won his way across the court and into the interior building. He passed up the broad staircase, and the voices and merriment of the revellers smote his ear at a distance. At the entrance of the reception-rooms he found a page, whom he despatched with a message to Zicci. The page did the errand; and the Corsican, on hearing the whispered name of Glyndon, turned to his host.

"Pardon me, my lord, an English friend of mine, the Signor Glyndon (not unknown by name to your Excellency), waits without. The business must indeed be urgent on which he has sought me in such an hour. You will forgive my momentary absence."

"Nay, signor," answered the Prince, courteously, but with a sinister smile on his countenance, "would it not be better for your friend to join us? An Englishman is welcome everywhere; and even were he a Dutchman, your friendship would invest his presence with attraction. Pray his attendance,—we would not spare you even for a moment."

Zicci bowed. The page was despatched with all flattering messages to Glyndon, a seat next to Zicci was placed for him, and the young Englishman entered.

"You are most welcome, sir. I trust your business to our illustrious guest is of good omen and pleasant import. If you bring evil news, defer it, I pray you."

Glyndon's brow was sullen, and he was about to startle the guests by his reply, when Zicci, touching his arm significantly, whispered in English, "I know why you have sought me. Be silent, and witness what ensues."

"You know, then, that Isabel, whom you boasted you had the power to save from danger—"

"Is in this house? Yes. I know also that Murder sits at the right hand of our host. Be still, and learn the fate that awaits the foes of Zicci."

"My lord," said the Corsican, speaking aloud, "the Signor Glyndon has indeed brought me tidings which, though not unexpected, are unwelcome. I learn that which will oblige me to leave Naples to-morrow, though I trust but for a short time. I have now a new motive to make the most of the present hour."

"And what, if I may venture to ask, may be the cause which brings such affliction on the fair dames of Naples?"

"It is the approaching death of one who honored me with most loyal friendship," replied Zicci, gravely. "Let us not speak of it,—Grief cannot put back the dial. As we supply by new flowers those that fade in our vases, so it is the secret of worldly wisdom to replace by fresh friendships those that fade from our path."

"True philosophy," exclaimed the Prince. "'Not to admire' was the Roman's maxim; never to mourn is mine. There is nothing in life to grieve for,—save, indeed, Signor Zicci, when some beauty on whom we have set our heart slips from our grasp. In such a moment we have need of all our wisdom not to succumb to despair and shake hands with death. What say you, signor? You smile. Such never could be your lot. Pledge me in a sentiment: 'Long life; to the fortunate lover; a quick release to the baffled suitor!'"

"I pledge you," said Zicci. And as the fatal wine was poured into his glass, he repeated, fixing his eyes on the Prince, "I pledge you even in this wine!"

He lifted the glass to his lips. The Prince seemed ghastly pale, while the gaze of the Corsican bent upon him with an intent and stern brightness that the conscience-stricken host cowered and quailed beneath. Not till he had drained the draught and replaced the glass upon the board did Zicci turn his eyes from the Prince; and he then said, "Your wine has been kept too long,—it has lost its virtues. It might disagree with many; but do not fear, it will not harm me, Prince. Signor Mascari, you are a judge of the grape, will you favor us with your opinion?"

"Nay," answered Mascari, with well-affected composure, "I like not the wines of Cyprus, they are heating. Perhaps Signor Glyndon may not have the same distaste. The English are said to love their potations warm and pungent."

"Do you wish my friend also to taste the wine, Prince?" said Zicci. "Recollect all cannot drink it with the same impunity as myself."

"No," said the Prince, hastily; "if you do not recommend the wine, Heaven forbid that we should constrain our guests! My Lord Duke," turning to one of the Frenchmen, "yours is the true soil of Bacchus. What think you of this cask from Burgundy,—has it borne the journey?"

"Ah!" said Zicci, "let us change both the wine and the theme." With that the Corsican grew more animated and brilliant. Never did wit more sparkling, airy, exhilarating, flash from the lips of reveller. His spirits fascinated all present, even the Prince himself, even Glyndon, with a strange and wild contagion. The former, indeed, whom the words and gaze of Zicci, when he drained the poison, had filled with fearful misgivings, now hailed in the brilliant eloquence of his wit a certain sign of the operation of the bane. The wine circulated fast, but none seemed conscious of its effects. One by one the rest of the party fell into a charmed and spell-bound silence as Zicci continued to pour forth sally upon sally, tale upon tale. They hung on his words, they almost held their breath to listen. Yet how bitter was his mirth; how full of contempt for all things; how deeply steeped in the coldness of the derision that makes sport of life itself!

Night came on; the room grew dim, and the feast had lasted several hours longer than was the customary duration of similar entertainments at that day. Still the guests stirred not, and still Zicci continued, with glittering eye and mocking lip, to lavish his stores of intellect and anecdote, when suddenly the moon rose, and shed its rays over the flowers and fountains in the court without, leaving the room itself half in shadow and half tinged by a quiet and ghostly light.

It was then that Zicci rose. "Well, gentlemen," said he, "we have not yet wearied our host, I hope, and his garden offers a new temptation to protract our stay. Have you no musicians among your train, Prince, that might regale our ears while we inhale the fragrance of your orange-trees?"

"An excellent thought," said the Prince. "Mascari, see to the music."

The party rose simultaneously to adjourn to the garden; and then, for the first time, the effect of the wine they had drunk seemed to make itself felt.

With flushed cheeks and unsteady steps they came into the open air, which tended yet more to stimulate that glowing fever of the grape. As if to make up for the silence with which the guests had hitherto listened to Zicci, every tongue was now loosened; every man talked, no man listened. In the serene beauty of the night and scene there was something wild and fearful in the contrast of the hubbub and Babel of these disorderly roysterers. One of the Frenchmen in especial, the young Due de R—,—a nobleman of the highest rank, and of all the quick, vivacious, and irascible temperament of his countrymen,—was particularly noisy and excited. And as circumstances, the remembrance of which is still preserved among certain circles of Naples, rendered it afterwards necessary that the Due should himself give evidence of what occurred, I will here translate the short account he drew up, and which was kindly submitted to me some few years ago by my accomplished and lively friend, il Cavaliere di B—.

I never remember [writes the Due] to have felt my spirits so excited as on that evening; we were like so many boys released from school, jostling each other as we reeled or ran down the flight of seven or eight stairs that led from the colonnade into the garden,—some laughing, some whooping, some scolding, some babbling. The wine had brought out, as it were, each man's inmost character. Some were loud and quarrelsome, others sentimental and whining; some, whom we had hitherto thought dull, most mirthful; some, whom we had ever regarded as discreet and taciturn, most garrulous and uproarious. I remember that in the midst of our most clamorous gayety my eye fell upon the foreign cavalier, Signor Zicci, whose conversation had so enchanted us all, and I felt a certain chill come over me to perceive that he bore the same calm and unsympathizing smile upon his countenance which had characterized it in his singular and curious stories of the court of Louis XV. I felt, indeed, half inclined to seek a quarrel with one whose composure was almost an insult to our disorder. Nor was such an effect of this irritating and mocking tranquillity confined to myself alone. Several of the party have told me since that on looking at Zicci they felt their blood rise and their hands wander to their sword-hilts. There seemed in the icy smile a very charm to wound vanity and provoke rage. It was at this moment that the Prince came up to me, and, passing his arm into mine, led me a little apart from the rest he had certainly indulged in the same excess as ourselves, but it did not produce the same effect of noisy excitement. There was, on the contrary a certain cold arrogance and supercilious scorn in his bearing and language, which, even while affecting so much caressing courtesy towards me, roused my self-love against him. He seemed as if Zicci had infected him, and that in imitating the manner of his guest he surpassed the original, he rallied me on some court gossip which had honored my name by associating it with a certain beautiful and distinguished Sicilian lady, and affected to treat with contempt that which, had it been true, I should have regarded as a boast. He spoke, indeed, as if he himself had gathered all the flowers of Naples, and left us foreigners only the gleanings he had scorned; at this my natural and national gallantry was piqued, and I retorted by some sarcasms that I should certainly have spared had my blood been cooler. He laughed heartily, and left me in a strange fit of resentment and anger. Perhaps (I must own the truth) the wine had produced in me a wild disposition to take offence and provoke quarrel. As the Prince left me, I turned, and saw Zicci at my side.

"The Prince is a braggart," said he, with the same smile that displeased me before. "He would monopolize all fortune and all love. Let us take our revenge."

"And how?"

"He has at this moment in his house the most enchanting singer in Naples,—the celebrated Isabel di Pisani. She is here, it is true, not by her own choice,—he carried her hither by force; but he will pretend to swear that she adores him. Let us insist on his producing the secret treasure; and when she enters, the Duc de Lt—can have no doubt that his flatteries and attentions will charm the lady and provoke all the jealous fears of our host. It would be a fair revenge upon his imperious self conceit."

This suggestion delighted me. I hastened to the Prince. At that instant the musicians had just commenced. I waved my hand, ordered the music to stop, and addressing the Prince, who was standing in the centre of one of the gayest groups, complained of his want of hospitality in affording to us such poor proficients in the art while he reserved for his own solace the lute and voice of the first performer in Naples. I demanded, half laughingly, half seriously, that he should produce the Pisani. My demand was received with shouts of applause by the rest. We drowned the replies of our host with uproar, and would hear no denial. "Gentlemen," at last said the Prince, when he could obtain an audience, "even were I to assent to your proposal, I could not induce the signora to present herself before an assemblage as riotous as they are noble. You have too much chivalry to use compulsion with her, though the Due de R—forgets himself sufficiently to administer it to inc."

I was stung by this taunt, however well deserved. "Prince," said I, "I have for the indelicacy of compulsion so illustrious an example that I cannot hesitate to pursue the path honored by your own footsteps. All Naples knows that the Pisani despises at once your gold and your love; that force alone could have brought her under your roof; and that you refuse to produce her because you fear her complaints, and know enough of the chivalry your vanity sneers at to feel assured that the gentlemen of France are not more disposed to worship beauty than to defend it from wrong."

"You speak well, sir," said Zicci, gravely;—"the Prince dare not produce his prize."

The Prince remained speechless for a few moments, as if with indignation. At last he broke out into expressions the most injurious and insulting against Signor Zicci and myself. Zicci replied not; I was more hot and hasty. The guests appeared to delight in our dispute. None except Mascari, whom we pushed aside and disdained to hear, strove to conciliate; some took one side, some another. The issue may be well foreseen. Swords were drawn. I had left mine in the ante room; Zicci offered me his own,—I seized it eagerly. There might be some six or eight persons engaged in a strange and confused kind of melee, but the Prince and myself only sought each other. The noise around us, the confusion of the guests, the cries of the musicians, the clash of our own swords, only served to stimulate our unhappy fury. We feared to be interrupted by the attendants and fought like madmen, without skill or method. I thrust and parried mechanically, blind and frantic as if a demon had entered into me, till I saw the Prince stretched at my feet, bathed in his blood, and Zicci bending over him and whispering in his ear. The sight cooled us all; the strife ceased. We gathered in shame, remorse, and horror round our ill-fated host; but it was too late, his eyes rolled fearfully in his head, and still he struggled to release himself from Zicci's arms, who continued to whisper (I trust divine comfort) in his ear. I have seen men die, but, never one who wore such horror on his countenance. At last all was over; Zicci rose from the corpse, and taking, with great composure, his sword from my hand,—"Ye are witnesses, gentlemen," said he, calmly, "that the Prince brought his fate upon himself. The last of that illustrious house has perished in a brawl."

I saw no more of Zicci. I hastened to the French ambassador to narrate the event and abide the issue. I am grateful to the Neapolitan government and to the illustrious heir of the unfortunate nobleman for the lenient and generous, yet just, interpretation put upon a misfortune the memory of which will afflict me to the last hour of my life. (Signed) Louis Victor, Duc de R.

In the above memorial the reader will find the most exact and minute account yet given of an event which created the most lively sensation at Naples in that day, and the narration of which first induced me to collect the materials of this history, which the reader will perceive, as it advances, is altogether different in its nature, its agencies, and its aims from those tales of external terror, whether derived from ingenious imposture or supernatural mystery, that have given life to French melodrama or German romance.

CHAPTER XVII

Glyndon had taken no part in the affray, neither had he participated largely in the excesses of the revel. For his exemption from both he was perhaps indebted to the whispered exhortations of Zicci. When the last rose from the corpse and withdrew from that scene of confusion, Glyndon remarked that in passing the crowd he touched Mascari on the shoulder, and said something which the Englishman did not overhear. Glyndon followed Zicci into the banquet-room, which, save where the moonlight slept on the marble floor, was wrapped in the sad and gloomy shadows of the advancing night.

"How could you foretell this fearful event? He fell not by your arm," said Glyndon, in a tremulous and hollow tone.

"The general who calculates on the victory does not fight in person," answered Zicci. "But enough of this. Meet me at midnight by the seashore, half a mile to the left of your hotel,—you will know the spot by a rude pillar, the only one near—, to which a broken chain is attached. There and then will be the crisis of your fate; go. I have business here yet,—remember, Isabel is still in the house of the dead man."

As Glyndon yet hesitated, strange thoughts, doubts, and fears that longed for speech crowding within him, Mascari approached; and Zicci, turning to the Italian and waving his hand to Glyndon, drew the former aside. Glyndon slowly departed.

"Mascari," said Zicci, "your patron is no more. Your services will be valueless to his heir,—a sober man, whom poverty has preserved from vice. For yourself, thank me that I do not give you up to the executioner,—recollect the wine of Cyprus. Well, never tremble, man, it could not act on me, though it might re-act on others,—in that it is a common type of crime. I forgive you; and if the wine should kill me, I promise you that my ghost shall not haunt so worshipful a penitent. Enough of this. Conduct me to the chamber of Isabel di Pisani; you have no further need of her. The death of the jailer opens the cell of the captive. Be quick,—I would be gone." Mascari muttered some inaudible words, bowed low, and led the way to the chamber in which Isabel was confined.

CHAPTER XVIII

It wanted several minutes of midnight, and Glyndon repaired to the appointed spot. The mysterious empire which Zicci had acquired over him was still more solemnly confirmed by the events of the last few hours; the sudden fate of the Prince, so deliberately foreshadowed, and yet so seemingly accidental—brought out by causes the most commonplace, and yet associated with words the most prophetic,—impressed him with the deepest sentiments of admiration and awe. It was as if this dark and wondrous being would convert the most ordinary events and the meanest instruments into the agencies of his inscrutable will; yet, if so, why have permitted the capture of Isabel? Why not have prevented the crime rather than punished the criminal? And did Zicci really feel love for Isabel? Love, and yet offer to resign her to himself,—to a rival whom his arts could not fail to baffle? He no longer reverted to the belief that Zicci or Isabel had sought to dupe him into marriage. His fear and reverence for the former now forbade the notion of so poor an imposture. Did he any longer love Isabel himself? No. When, that morning, he heard of her danger, he had, it is true, returned to the sympathies and the fears of affection; but with the death of the Prince her image faded again from his heart, and he felt no jealous pang at the thought that she had been saved by Zicci,—that at that moment she was perhaps beneath his roof. Whoever has, in the course of his life, indulged the absorbing passion of the gamester, will remember bow all other pursuits and objects vanished from his mind, how solely he was wrapped in the one wild delusion; with what a sceptre of magic power the despot demon ruled every feeling and every thought. Far more intense than the passion of the gamester was the frantic yet sublime desire that mastered the breast of Glyndon. He would be the rival of Zicci, not in human and perishable affections, but in preternatural and eternal lore. He would have laid down life with content, nay, rapture, as the price of learning those solemn secrets which separated the stranger from mankind.. Such fools are we when we aspire to be over-wise! To be enamoured too madly of the goddess of goddesses is only to embrace a cloud, and to forfeit alike heaven and earth.

The night was most lovely and serene, and the waves scarcely rippled at his feet as the Englishman glided on by the cool and starry beach. At length he arrived at the spot, and there, leaning against the broken pillar, he beheld a man wrapped in a long mantle and in an attitude of profound repose. He approached, and uttered the name of Zicci. The figure turned, and he saw the face of a stranger,—a face not stamped by the glorious beauty of the Corsican, but equally majestic in its aspect, and perhaps still more impressive from the mature age and the passionless depth of thought that characterized the expanded forehead and deep-set but piercing eyes.

"You seek Zicci," said the stranger,—"he will be here anon; but perhaps he whom you see before you is more connected with your destiny, and more disposed to realize your dreams."

"Hath the earth then another Zicci?"

"If not," replied the stranger, "why do you cherish the hope and the wild faith to be yourself a Zicci? Think you that none others have burned with the same godlike dream? Who, indeed, in his first youth;—youth, when the soul is nearer to the heaven from which it sprang, and its divine and primal longings are not all effaced by the sordid passions and petty cares that are begot in time?—who is there in youth that has not nourished the belief that the universe has secrets not known to the common herd, and panted, as the hart for the water-springs, for the fountains that he hid and far away amidst the broad wilderness of trackless science? The music of the fountain is heard in the soul within till the steps, deceived and erring, rove away from its waters, and the wanderer dies in the mighty desert. Think you that none who have cherished the hope have found the truth, or that the yearning after the Ineffable Knowledge was given to us utterly in vain? No. Every desire in human hearts is but a glimpse of things that exist, alike distant and divine. No! in the world there have been, from age to age, some brighter and happier spirits who have won to the air in which the beings above mankind move and breathe. Zicci, great though he be, stands not alone; he has his predecessors, his contemporary rivals, and long lines of successors are yet to come!"

"And will you tell me," said Glyndon, "that in yourself I behold one of that mighty few over whom Zicci has no superiority in power and wisdom?"

"In me," answered the stranger, "you see one from whom Zicci himself learned many of his loftiest secrets. Before his birth my wisdom was! On these shores, on this spot, have I stood in ages that your chronicles but feebly reach. The Phoenician, the Greek, the Oscan, the Roman, the Lombard,—I have seen them all!—leaves gay and glittering on the trunk of the universal life—scattered in due season and again renewed; till, indeed, the same race that gave its glory to the ancient world bestowed a second youth on the new. For the pure Greeks—the Hellenes, whose origin has bewildered your dreaming scholars—were of the same great family as the Norman tribe, born to be the lords of the universe, and in no land on earth destined to be the hewers of wood. Even the dim traditions of the learned that bring the sons of Hellas from the vast and undetermined territories of Northern Thrace, to be the victors of the pastoral Pelasgi, and the founders of the line of demi-gods, might serve you to trace back their primeval settlements to the same region whence, in later times, the Norman warriors broke on the dull and savage hordes of the Celt, and became the Greeks of the Christian world. But this interests you not, and you are wise in your indifference. Not in the knowledge of things without, but in the perfection of the soul within, lies the empire of man aspiring to be more than men."

"And what books contain that science; from what laboratory is it wrought?"

"Nature supplies the materials: they are around you in your daily walks; in the herbs that the beast devours and the chemist disdains to cull; in the elements, from which matter in its meanest and its mightiest shapes is deduced; in the wide bosom of the air; in the black abysses of the earth,—everywhere are given to mortals the resources and libraries of immortal lore. But as the simplest problems in the simplest of all studies are obscure to one who braces not his mind to their comprehension; as the rower in yonder vessel cannot tell you why two circles can touch each other only in one point,—so, though all earth were carved over and inscribed with the letters of diviner knowledge, the characters would be valueless to him who does not pause to inquire the language and meditate the truth. Young man, if thy imagination is vivid; if thy heart is daring, if thy curiosity is insatiate, I will accept thee as my pupil. But the first lessons are stern and dread."

"If thou hast mastered them, why not I?" answered Glyndon, boldly. "I have felt from my boyhood that strange mysteries were reserved for my career, and from the proudest ends of ordinary ambition I have carried my gaze into the cloud and darkness that stretch beyond. The instant I beheld Zicci, I felt as if I had discovered the guide and the tutor for which my youth had idly languished and vainly burned."

"And to me his duty can be transferred," replied the stranger. "Yonder lies, anchored in the bay, the vessel in which Zicci seeks a fairer home; a little while and the breeze will rise, the sail will swell, and the stranger will have passed like a wind away. Still, like the wind, he leaves in thy heart the seeds that may bear the blossom and the fruit. Zicci hath performed his task—he is wanted no more; the perfecter of his work is at thy side. He comes—I hear the dash of the oar. You will have your choice submitted to you. According as you decide, we shall meet again." With these words the stranger moved slowly away, and disappeared beneath the shadow of the cliffs. A boat glided rapidly across the waters; it touched land, a man leapt on shore, and Glyndon recognized Zicci.

"I give thee, Glyndon, I give thee no more the option of happy love and serene enjoyment. That hour is past, and fate has linked the hand that might have been thine own to mine. But I have ample gifts to bestow upon thee if thou wilt abandon the hope that gnaws thy heart, and the realization of which even I have not the power to foresee. Be thine ambition human, and I can gratify it to the full. Men desire four things in life,—love, wealth, fame, power. The first I cannot give thee,—no matter why; the rest are at my disposal. Select which of them thou wilt, and let us part in peace."

"Such are not the gifts I covet: I choose knowledge, which indeed, as the schoolman said, is power, and the loftiest; that knowledge must be thine own. For this, and for this alone, I surrendered the love of Isabel; this, and this alone, must be any recompense."

"I cannot gainsay thee, though I can warn. The desire to learn does not always contain the faculty to acquire. I can give thee, it is true, the teacher; the rest must depend on thee. Be wise in time, and take that which I can assure to thee."

"Answer me but these questions, and according to your answer I will decide. Is it in the power of man to attain intercourse with the beings of other worlds? Is it in the power of man to read the past and the future, and to insure life against the sword and against disease?"

"All this may be possible," answered Zicci evasively, "to the few. But for one who attains such secrets, millions may perish in the attempt."

"One question more. Thou—"

"Beware! Of myself, as I have said before, I render no account."

"Well, then, the stranger I have met this night—are his boasts to be believed? Is he in truth one of the chosen seers whom you allow to have mastered the mysteries I yearn to fathom?"

"Rash man," said Zicci, in a tone of compassion, "thy crisis is past, and thy choice made. I can only bid thee be bold and prosper. Yes, I resign thee to a master who has the power and the will to open to thee the gates of the awful world. Thy weal or woe are as nought in the eyes of his relentless wisdom. I would bid him spare thee, but he will heed me not. Mejnour, receive thy pupil!" Glyndon turned, and his heart beat when he perceived that the stranger, whose footsteps he had not heard on the pebbles, whose approach he had not beheld in the moonlight, was once more by his side.

Glyndon's eyes followed the receding form of the mysterious Corsican. He saw him enter the boat, and he then for the first time noticed that besides the rowers there was a female, who stood up as Zicci gained the boat. Even at this distance he recognized the once-adored form of Isabel. She waved her hand to him, and across the still and shining air came her voice, mournfully and sweetly in her native tongue, "Farewell, Clarence—farewell, farewell."

He strove to answer, but the voice touched a chord at his heart, and the words failed him. Isabel was then lost forever,—gone with this dread stranger,—darkness was round her lot. And he himself had decided her fate and his own! The boat bounded on, the soft waves flashed and sparkled beneath the oars, and it was along one sapphire track of moonlight that the frail vessel bore away the lovers. Farther and farther from his gaze sped the boat, till at last the speck, scarcely visible, touched the side of the ship that lay lifeless in the glorious bay. At that instant, as if by magic, up sprang with a glad murmur the playful and refreshing wind. And Glyndon turned to Mejnour, and broke the silence.

"Tell me,—if thou canst read the future,—tell me that her lot will be fair, and that her choice at least is wise."

"My pupil," answered Mejnour, in a voice the calmness of which well accorded with the chilling words, "thy first task must be to withdraw all thought, feeling, sympathy from others. The elementary stage of knowledge is to make self, and self alone, thy study and thy world. Thou hast decided thine own career; thou hast renounced love; thou hast rejected wealth, fame, and the vulgar pomps of power. What, then, are all mankind to thee? To perfect thy faculties and concentrate thy emotions is henceforth thy only aim."

"And will happiness be the end?"

"If happiness exist," answered Mejnour, "it must be centred in A Self to which all passion is unknown. But happiness is the last state of being, and as yet thou art on the threshold of the first!"

As Mejnour spoke, the distant vessel spread its sails to the wind, and moved slowly along the deep. Glyndon sighed, and the pupil and the master retraced their steps towards the city.

BOOK II

CHAPTER I

It was about a month after the date of Zicci's departure and Glyndon's introduction to Mejnour, when two Englishmen were walking arm-in-arm through the Toledo.

"I tell you," said one (who spoke warmly), "that if you have a particle of common-sense left in you, you will accompany me to England. This Mejnour is an impostor more dangerous—because more in earnest—than Zicci. After all, what do his promises amount to? You allow that nothing can be more equivocal. You say that he has left Naples, that he has selected a retreat more genial than the crowded thoroughfares of men to the studies in which he is to initiate you; and this retreat is among the haunts of the fiercest bandits of Italy,—haunts which Justice itself dare not penetrate; fitting hermitage for a sage! I tremble for you. What if this stranger, of whom nothing is known, be leagued with the robbers; and these lures for your credulity bait but the traps for your property,—perhaps your life? You might come off cheaply by a ransom of half your fortune; you smile indignantly well! put common-sense out of the question; take your own view of the matter. You are to undergo an ordeal which Mejnour himself does not profess to describe as a very tempting one. It may, or it may not, succeed; if it does not, you are menaced with the darkest evils; and if it does, you cannot be better off than the dull and joyless mystic whom you have taken for a master. Away with this folly! Enjoy youth while it is left to you. Return with me to England; forget these dreams. Enter your proper career; form affections more respectable than those which lured you a while to an Italian adventuress, and become a happy and distinguished man. This is the advice of sober friendship; yet the promises I hold out to you are fairer than those of Mejnour."

"Merton," said Glyndon, doggedly, "I cannot, if I would, yield to your wishes. A power that is above me urges me on; I cannot resist its fascination. I will proceed to the last in the strange career I have commenced. Think of me no more. Follow yourself the advice you give to me, and be happy."

"This is madness," said Merton, passionately, but with a tear in his eye; "your health is already failing; you are so changed I should scarcely know you: come, I have already had your name entered in my passport; in another hour I shall be gone, and you, boy that you are, will be left without a friend to the deceits of your own fancy and the machinations of this relentless mountebank."

"Enough," said Glyndon, coldly; "you cease to be an effective counsellor when you suffer your prejudices to be thus evident. I have already had ample proof," added the Englishman, and his pale cheek grew more pale, "of the power of this man,—if man he be, which I sometimes doubt; and, come life, come death, I will not shrink from the paths that allure me. Farewell, Merton: if we never meet again; if you hear amidst our old and cheerful haunts that Clarence Glyndon sleeps the last sleep by the shores of Naples, or amidst the Calabrian hills,—say to the friends of our youth, 'He died worthily, as thousands of martyr-students have died before him, in the pursuit of knowledge.'"

He wrung Merton's hand as he spoke, darted from his side, and disappeared amidst the crowd.

That day Merton left Naples; the next morning Glyndon also quitted the City of Delight, alone and on horseback. He bent his way into those picturesque but dangerous parts of the country which at that time were infested by banditti, and which few travellers dared to pass, even in broad daylight, without a strong escort. A road more lonely cannot well be conceived than that on which the hoofs of his steed, striking upon the fragments of rock that encumbered the neglected way, woke a dull and melancholy echo. Large tracts of waste land, varied by the rank and profuse foliage of the South, lay before him; occasionally a wild goat peeped down from some rocky crag, or the discordant cry of a bird of prey, startled in its sombre haunt, was heard above the hills. These were the only signs of life; not a human being was met, not a hut was visible. Wrapped in his own ardent and solemn thoughts, the young man continued his way, till the sun had spent its noonday heat, and a breeze that announced the approach of eve sprung up from the unseen ocean that lay far distant to his sight. It was then that a turn in the road brought before him one of those long, desolate, gloomy villages which are found in the interior of the Neapolitan dominions; and now he came upon a small chapel on one side of the road, with a gaudily painted image of the Virgin in the open shrine. Around this spot, which in the heart of a Christian land retained the vestige of the old idolatry (for just such were the chapels that in the Pagan age were dedicated to the demon-saints of mythology), gathered six or seven miserable and squalid wretches, whom the Curse of the Leper had cut off from mankind. They set up a shrill cry as they turned their ghastly visages towards the horseman; and, without stirring from the spot, stretched out their gaunt arms, and implored charity in the name of the Merciful Mother. Glyndon hastily threw them some small coins, and, turning away his face, clapped spurs to his horse, and relaxed not his speed till he entered the village. On either side the narrow and miry street, fierce and haggard forms—some leaning against the ruined walls of blackened huts, some seated at the threshold, some lying at full length in the mud—presented groups that at once invoked pity and aroused alarm; pity for their squalor,—alarm for the ferocity imprinted on their savage aspects. They gazed at him, grim and sullen, as he rode slowly up the rugged street; sometimes whispering significantly to each other, but without attempting to stop his way. Even the children hushed their babble, and ragged urchins, devouring him with sparkling eyes, muttered to their mothers, "We shall feast well to-morrow!" It was, indeed, one of those hamlets in which Law sets not its sober step, in which Violence and Murder house secure,—hamlets common then in the wilder parts of Italy, in which the peasant was but the gentler name for the robber.

Glyndon's heart somewhat failed him as he looked around, and the question he desired to ask died upon his lips. At length, from one of the dismal cabins emerged a form superior to the rest. Instead of the patched and ragged overall which made the only garment of the men he had hitherto seen, the dress of this person was characterized by all the trappings of Calabrian bravery. Upon his raven hair, the glossy curls of which made a notable contrast to the matted and elfin locks of the savages around, was placed a cloth cap with a gold tassel that hung down to his shoulder; his mustaches were trimmed with care, and a silk kerchief of gay lines was twisted round a well-shaped but sinewy throat; a short jacket of rough cloth was decorated with several rows of gilt filagree buttons; his nether garments fitted tight to his limbs, and were curiously braided; while in a broad, party-colored sash were placed four silver-hilted pistols; and the sheathed knife, usually worn by Italians of the lower order, was mounted in ivory elaborately carved. A small carbine of handsome workmanship was slung across his shoulder, and completed his costume. The man himself was of middle size, athletic, yet slender; with straight and regular features,—sunburnt, but not swarthy; and an expression of countenance which, though reckless and bold, had in it frankness rather than ferocity, and, if defying, was not altogether unprepossessing.

Glyndon, after eyeing this figure for some moments with great attention, checked his rein, and asked in the provincial patois, with which he was tolerably familiar, the way to the "Castle of the Mountain."

The man lifted his cap as he heard the question, and, approaching Glyndon, laid his hand upon the neck of the horse, and said in a low voice, "Then you are the cavalier whom our patron the signor expected. He bade me wait for you here, and lead you to the castle. And indeed, signor, it might have been unfortunate if I had neglected to obey the command." The man then, drawing a little aside, called out to the bystanders in a loud voice, "Ho, ho, my friends, pay henceforth and forever all respect to this worshipful cavalier. He is the accepted guest of our blessed patron of the Castle of the Mountain. Long life to him! May he, like his host, be safe by day and by night, in the hill and on the waste, against the dagger and the bullet, in limb and in life! Cursed be he who touches a hair of his head, or a baioccho in his pouch. Now and forever we will protect and honor him; for the law or against the law; with the faith, and to the death. Amen. Amen!"

"Amen!" responded in wild chorus a hundred voices, and the scattered and straggling groups pressed up the street, nearer and nearer to the horseman.

"And that he may be known," continued the Englishman's strange protector, "to the eye and to the ear, I place around him the white sash, and I give him the sacred watchword,—'Peace to the Brave.' Signor, when you wear this sash, the proudest in these parts will bare the head and bend the knee. Signor, when you utter this watchword, the bravest hearts will be bound to your bidding. Desire you safety, or ask you revenge; to gain a beauty, or to lose a foe, speak but the word, and we are yours, we are yours! Is it not so, comrades?" And again the hoarse voices shouted, "Amen, amen!"

"Now, signor," whispered the bravo, in good Italian, "if you have a few coins to spare, scatter them amongst the crowd, and let us be gone."

Glyndon, not displeased at the concluding sentence, emptied his purse in the street; and while, with mingled oaths, blessings, shrieks, and yells, men, women, and children scrambled for the money, the bravo, taking the rein of the horse, led it a few paces through the village at a brisk trot, and then turning up a narrow lane to the left, in a few minutes neither houses nor men were visible, and the mountains closed their path on either side. It was then that, releasing the bridle and slackening his pace, the guide turned his dark eyes on Glyndon with an arch expression, and said,—

"Your Excellency was not, perhaps, prepared for the hearty welcome we have given you."

"Why, in truth, I ought to have been prepared for it, since my friend, to whose house I am bound, did not disguise from me the character of the neighborhood. And your name, my friend, if I may call you so?"

"Oh, no ceremonies with me, Excellency. In the village I am generally called Maestro Paulo. I had a surname once, though a very equivocal one; and I have forgotten that since I retired from the world."

"And was it from disgust, from poverty, or from some some ebullition of passion which entailed punishment, that you betook yourself to the mountains?"

"Why, signor," said the bravo, with a gay laugh, "hermits of my class seldom love the confessional. However, I have no secrets while my step is in these defiles, my whistle in my pouch, and my carbine at my back." With that the robber, as if he loved permission to talk at his will, hemmed thrice, and began with much humor; though, as his tale proceeded, the memories it roused seemed to carry him further than he at first intended, and reckless and light-hearted ease gave way to that fierce and varied play of countenance and passion of gesture which characterize the emotions of his countrymen.

"I was born at Terracina,—a fair spot, is it not? My father was a learned monk, of high birth; my mother—Heaven rest her!—an innkeeper's pretty daughter. Of course there was no marriage in the case; and when I was born, the monk gravely declared my appearance to be miraculous. I was dedicated from my cradle to the altar; and my head was universally declared to be the orthodox shape for a cowl. As I grew up, the monk took great pains with my education, and I learned Latin and psalmody as soon as less miraculous infants learn crowing. Nor did the holy man's care stint itself to my interior accomplishments. Although vowed to poverty, he always contrived that my mother should have her pockets full; and between her pockets and mine there was soon established a clandestine communication; accordingly, at fourteen, I wore my cap on one side, stuck pistols in my belt, and assumed the swagger of a cavalier and a gallant. At that age my poor mother died; and about the same period, my father, having written a 'History of the Pontifical Bulls,' in forty volumes, and being, as I said, of high birth, obtained a cardinal's hat. From that time he thought fit to disown your humble servant. He bound me over to an honest notary at Naples, and gave me two hundred crowns by way of provision. Well, signor, I saw enough of the law to convince me that I should never be rogue enough to shine in the profession. So instead of spoiling parchment, I made love to the notary's daughter. My master discovered our innocent amusement, and turned me out of doors,—that was disagreeable. But my Ninetta loved me, and took care that I should not lie out in the streets with the lazzaroni. Little jade, I think I see her now, with her bare feet, and her finger to her lips, opening the door in the summer nights, and bidding me creep softly into the kitchen, where—praised be the saints!—a flask and a manchet always awaited the hungry amoroso. At last, however, Ninetta grew cold. It is the way of the sex, signor. Her father found her an excellent marriage in the person of a withered picture-dealer. She took the spouse, and very properly clapped the door in the face of the lover. I was not disheartened, Excellency; no, not I. Women are plentiful while we are young. So, without a ducat in my pocket, or a crust for my teeth, I set out to seek my fortune on board of a Spanish merchantman. That was duller work than I expected: but luckily we were attacked by a pirate; half the crew were butchered, the rest captured. I was one of the last,—always in luck, you see, signor, monks' sons have a knack that way! The captain of the pirate took a fancy to me. 'Serve with us,' said he. 'Too happy,' said I. Behold me then a pirate. Oh jolly life! how I blest the old notary for turning me out of doors! What feasting! what fighting! what wooing! what quarreling! Sometimes we ran ashore and enjoyed ourselves like princes; sometimes we lay in a calm for days together, on the loveliest sea that man ever traversed. And then, if the breeze rose, and a sail came in sight, who so merry as we? I passed three years in that charming profession, and then, signor, I grew ambitious. I caballed against the captain; I wanted his post. One still night we struck the blow. The ship was like a log in the sea,—no land to be seen from the mast-head, the waves like glass, and the moon at its full. Up we rose,—thirty of us and more. Up we rose with a shout; we poured into the captain's cabin,—I at the head. The brave old boy had caught the alarm, and there he stood at the doorway, a pistol in each hand; and his one eye (he had only one) worse to meet than the pistols were.

"'Yield,' cried I, 'your life shall be safe.'

"'Take that,' said he, and whiz went the pistol; but the saints took care of their own, and the ball passed by my cheek, and shot the boatswain behind me. I closed with the captain, and the other pistol went off without mischief in the struggle; such a fellow he was, six feet four without his shoes! Over we went, rolling each on the other. Santa Maria!—no time to get hold of one's knife. Meanwhile, all the crew were up, some for the captain, some for me; clashing and firing, and swearing and groaning, and now and then a heavy splash in the sea! Fine supper for the sharks that night! At last old Bilboa got uppermost: out flashed his knife; down it came, but not in my heart. No! I gave my left arm as a shield, and the blade went through and through up to the hilt, with the blood spurting up like the rain from a whale's nostril. With the weight of the blow the stout fellow came down, so that his face touched mine; with my right hand I caught him by the throat, turned him over like a lamb, signor, and faith it was soon all up with him; the boatswain's brother, a fat Dutchman, ran him through with a pike.

"'Old fellow,' said I, as he turned up his terrible eye to me, 'I bear you no malice, but we must try to get on in the world, you know.' The captain grinned and gave up the ghost. I went upon deck; what a sight! Twenty bold fellows stark and cold, and the moon sparkling on the puddles of blood as calmly as if it were water. Well, signor, the victory was ours, and the ship mine; I ruled merrily enough for six months. We then attacked a French ship twice our size; what sport it was! And we had not had a good fight so long we were quite like virgins at it! We got the best of it, and won ship and cargo. They wanted to pistol the captain: but that was against my laws; so we gagged him, for he scolded as loud as if we were married to him; left him and the rest of his crew on board our own vessel, which was terribly battered:

clapped our black flag on the Frenchman's, and set off merrily, with a brisk wind in our favor. But luck deserted us on forsaking our own dear old ship. A storm came on; a plank struck; several of us escaped in the boats; we had lots of gold with us, but no water. For two days and two nights we suffered horribly: but at last we ran ashore near a French seaport; our sorry plight moved compassion, and as we had money we were not suspected; people only suspect the poor. Here we soon recovered our fatigues, rigged ourselves out gayly, and your humble servant was considered as noble a captain as ever walked deck. But now, alas, my fate would have it that I should fall in love with a silk-mercer's daughter. Ah! how I loved her,—the pretty Clara! Yes, I loved her so well, that I was seized with horror at my past life; I resolved to repent, to marry her, and settle down into an honest man. Accordingly, I summoned my messmates, told them my resolution, resigned my command, and persuaded them to depart. They were good fellows; engaged with a Dutchman, against whom I heard afterwards they made a successful mutiny, but I never saw them more. I had two thousand crowns still left; with this sum I obtained the consent of the silk-mercer, and it was agreed that I should become a partner in the firm. I need not say that no one suspected I had been so great a man, and I passed for a Neapolitan goldsmith's son instead of a cardinal's. I was very happy then, signor, very,—I could not have harmed a fly. Had I married Clara I had been as gentle a mercer as ever handled a measure."

The bravo paused a moment, and it was easy to see that he felt more than his words and tone betokened. "Well, well, we must not look back at the Past too earnestly,—the sun light upon it makes one's eyes water. The day was fixed for our wedding, it approached; on the evening before the appointed day, Clara, her mother, her little sister, and myself were walking by the port, and as we looked on the sea I was telling them old gossip tales of mermaids and sea-serpents,—when a red-faced bottle-nosed Frenchman clapped himself right before me, and placing his spectacles very deliberately astride his proboscis, echoed out, 'Sacre, mille tonnerres! This is the damned pirate that boarded the "Niobe"!'"

"None of your jests,' said I, mildly. 'Ho, ho,' said he. 'I can't be mistaken. Help there,' and he gripped me by the collar. I replied, as you may suppose, by laying him in the kennel; but it would not do. The French captain had a French lieutenant at his back, whose memory was as good as his master's. A crowd assembled; other sailors came up; the odds were against me. I slept that night in prison; and, in a few weeks afterwards, I was sent to the galleys. They had spared my life because the old Frenchman politely averred that I had made my crew spare his. You may believe that the oar and the chain were not to my taste. I, and two others, escaped; they took to the road, and have, no doubt, been long since broken on the wheel. I, soft soul, would not commit another crime to gain my bread, for Clara was still at my heart with her soft eyes; so, limiting my rogueries to the theft of a beggar's rags, which I compensated him by leaving my galley attire instead, I begged my way to the town where I left Clara. It was a clear winter's day when I approached the outskirts of the town. I had no fear of detection, for my beard and hair were as good as a mask. Oh, Mother of Mercy! there came across my way a funeral procession! There, now, you know it. I can tell you no more. She had died, perhaps of love, more likely of shame. Do you know how I spent that night? I will tell you; I stole a pickaxe from a mason's shed, and, all alone and unseen, under the frosty heavens I dug the fresh mould from the grave; I lifted the coffin; I wrenched the lid, I saw her again—again. Decay had not touched her. She was always pale in her life! I could have sworn she lived! It was a blessed thing to see her once more,—and all alone too! But then at dawn, to give her back to the earth,—to close the lid, to throw down the mould, to hear the pebbles rattle on the coffin,—that was dreadful! Signor, I never knew before, and I don't wish to think now, how valuable a thing human life is. At sunrise I was again a wanderer; but now that Clara was gone my scruples vanished, and again I was at war with my betters. I contrived, at last, at O—, to get taken on board a vessel bound to Leghorn, working out my passage. From Leghorn I went to Rome, and stationed myself at the door of the cardinal's palace. Out he came,—his gilded coach at the gate. "'Ho, father,' said I, 'don't you know me?'

"'Who are you?'

"'Your son,' said I, in a whisper.

"The cardinal drew back, looked at me earnestly, and mused a moment. 'All men are my sons,' quoth he then, very mildly; 'there is gold for thee. To him who begs once, alms are due; to him who begs twice, jails are open. Take the hint and molest me no more. Heaven bless thee!' With that he got into his coach and drove off to the Vatican. His purse, which he had left behind, was well supplied. I was grateful and contented, and took my way to Terracina. I had not long passed the marshes, when I saw two horsemen approach at a canter.

"'You look poor, friend,' said one of them, halting; 'yet you are strong.'

"'Poor men and strong are both serviceable and dangerous, Signor Cavalier.'

"'Well said! follow us.'

"I obeyed and became a bandit. I rose by degrees; and as I have always been mild in my calling, and have taken purses without cutting throats, bear an excellent character, and can eat my macaroni at Naples without any danger to life and limbs. For the last two years I have settled in these parts, where I hold sway, and where I have purchased land. I am called a farmer, signor; and I myself now only rob for amusement, and to keep my hand in. I trust I have satisfied your curiosity. We are within a hundred yards of the castle."

"And how," asked the Englishman, whose interest had been much excited by his companion's narrative, "and how came you acquainted with my host? and by what means has he so well conciliated the goodwill of yourself and your friends?"

Maestro Paulo turned his black eyes gravely towards his questioner. "Why, signor," said he, "you must surely know more of the foreign cavalier with the hard name than I do. All I can say is, that about a fortnight ago I chanced to be standing by a booth in the Toledo at Naples, when a sober-looking gentleman touched me by the arm, and said, 'Maestro Paulo, I want to make your acquaintance; do me the favor to come into yonder tavern.' When we were seated, my new acquaintance thus accosted me: 'The Count d' O—has offered to let me hire his old castle near B—. You know the spot?'

"'Extremely well; no one has inhabited it for a century at least; it is half in ruins, signor. A queer place to hire; I hope the rent is not heavy.'

"'Maestro Paulo,' said he, 'I am a philosopher, and don't care for luxuries. I want a quiet retreat for some scientific experiments. The castle will suit me very well, provided you will accept me as a neighbor, and place me and my friends under your special protection. I am rich; but I shall take nothing to the castle worth robbing. I will pay one rent to the count, and another to you.'

"With that we soon came to terms, and as the strange signor doubled the sum I myself proposed, he is in high favor with all his neighbors. We would guard the old castle against an army. And now, signor, that I have been thus frank, be frank with me. Who is this singular cavalier?"

"Who?—he himself told you, a philosopher."

"Hem! Searching for the philosopher's stone, eh? A bit of a magician; afraid of the priests?"

"Precisely. You have hit it."

"I thought so; and you are his pupil?"

"I am."

"I wish you well through it," said the robber, seriously, and crossing himself with much devotion; "I am not much better than other people, but one's soul is one's soul. I do not mind a little honest robbery, or knocking a man on the head if need be,—but to make a bargain with the devil!—Ah! take care, young gentleman, take care."

"You need not fear," said Glyndon, smiling; "my preceptor is too wise and too good for such a compact. But here we are, I suppose. A noble ruin! A glorious prospect!"

Glyndon paused delightedly, and surveyed the scene before and below with the eye of a poet and a painter. Insensibly, while listening to the bandit, he had wound up a considerable ascent, and now he was upon a broad ledge of rock covered with mosses and dwarf shrubs. Between this eminence and another of equal height, upon which the castle was built, there was a deep but narrow fissure, overgrown with the most profuse foliage, so that the eye could not penetrate many yards below the rugged surface of the abyss; but the profoundness might well be conjectured by the hoarse, low, monotonous sound of waters unseen that rolled below, and the subsequent course of which was visible at a distance in a perturbed and rapid stream that intersected the waste and desolate valleys. To the left, the prospect seemed almost boundless; the extreme clearness of the purple air serving to render distinct the features of a range of country that a conqueror of old might have deemed in itself a kingdom. Lonely and desolate as the road which Glyndon had passed that day had appeared, the landscape now seemed studded with castles, spires, and villages. Afar off, Naples gleamed whitely in the last rays of the sun, and the rose-tints of the horizon melted into the azure of her glorious bay. Yet more remote, and in another part of the prospect, might be caught, dim and shadowy, and backed by the darkest foliage, the ruined village of the ancient Possidonia. There, in the midst of his blackened and sterile realms, rose the dismal Mount of Fire; while, on the other hand, winding through variegated plains, to which distance lent all its magic, glittered many a stream, by which Etruscan and Sybarite, Roman and Saracen and Norman, had, at intervals of ages, pitched the invading tent. All the visions of the past the stormy and dazzling histories of Southern Italy—rushed over the artist's mind as he gazed below. And then, slowly turning to look behind, he saw the gray and mouldering walls of the castle in which he sought the secrets that were to give to hope in the Future a mightier empire than memory owns in the Past. It was one of those baronial fortresses with which Italy was studded in the earlier middle ages, having but little of the Gothic grace of grandeur which belongs to the ecclesiastical architecture of the same time; but rude, vast, and menacing even in decay. A wooden bridge was thrown over the chasm, wide enough to admit two horsemen abreast; and the planks trembled and gave back a hollow sound as Glyndon urged his jaded steed across.

A road that had once been broad, and paved with rough flags, but which now was half obliterated by long grass and rank weeds, conducted to the outer court of the castle hard by; the gates were open, and half the building in this part was dismantled, the ruins partially hid by ivy that was the growth of centuries. But on entering the inner court, Glyndon was not sorry to notice that there was less appearance of neglect and decay: some wild roses gave a smile to the gray walls; and in the centre there was a fountain, in which the waters still trickled coolly, and with a pleasing murmur, from the jaws of a gigantic triton. Here he was met by Mejnour with a smile.

"Welcome, my friend and pupil," said he; "he who seeks for Truth can find in these solitudes an immortal Academe."

CHAPTER II

The attendants which Mejnour had engaged for his strange abode were such as might suit a philosopher of few wants. An old Armenian, whom Glyndon recognized as in the mystic's service at Naples; a tall, hard-featured woman from the village, recommended by Maestro Paulo; and two long-haired, smooth-spoken, but fierce-visaged youths, from the same place, and honored by the same sponsorship,—constituted the establishment. The rooms used by the sage were commodious and weather-proof, with some remains of ancient splendor in the faded arras that clothed the walls and the huge tables of costly marble and elaborate carving. Glyndon's sleeping apartment communicated with a kind of belvidere or terrace that commanded prospects of unrivalled beauty and extent, and was separated, on the other side, by a long gallery and a flight of ten or a dozen stairs, from the private chambers of the mystic. There was about the whole place a sombre, and yet not displeasing, depth of repose. It suited well with the studies to which it was now to be appropriated.

For several days Mejnour refused to confer with Glyndon on the subjects nearest to his heart.

"All without," said he, "is prepared, but not all within. Your own soul must grow accustomed to the spot, and filled with the surrounding Nature; for Nature is the source of all inspiration."

With these words, which savored a little of jargon, Mejnour turned to lighter topics. He made the Englishman accompany him in long rambles through the wild scenes around, and he smiled approvingly when the young artist gave way to the enthusiasm which their fearful beauty could not have failed to rouse in a duller breast; and then Mejnour poured forth to his wondering pupil the stores of a knowledge that seemed inexhaustible and boundless. He gave accounts the most curious, graphic, and minute, of the various races—their characters, habits, creeds, and manners—by which that fair land had been successively overrun. It is true that his descriptions could not be found in books, and were unsupported by learned authorities; but he possessed the true charm of the tale-teller, and spoke of all with the animated confidence of a personal witness. Sometimes, too, he would converse upon the more durable and the loftier mysteries of Nature with an eloquence and a research which invested them with all the colors rather of poetry than science. Insensibly the young artist found himself elevated and soothed by the lore of his companion; the fever of his wild desires was slaked. His mind became more and more lulled into the divine tranquillity of contemplation; he felt himself a nobler being; and in the silence of his senses he imagined that he heard the voice of his soul.

It was to this state that Mejnour sought to bring the Neophyte, and in this elementary initiation the mystic was like every more ordinary sage. For he who seeks to discover must first reduce himself into a kind of abstract idealism, and be rendered up; in solemn and sweet bondage, to the faculties which contemplate and imagine.

Glyndon noticed that, in their rambles, Mejnour often paused where the foliage was rifest, to gather some herb or flower; and this reminded him that he had seen Zicci similarly occupied. "Can these humble children of Nature," said he one day to Mejnour, "things that bloom and wither in a day, be serviceable to the science of the higher secrets? Is there a pharmacy for the soul as well as the body, and do the nurslings of the summer minister not only to human health but spiritual immortality?"

"If," answered Mejnour, "before one property of herbalism was known to them, a stranger had visited a wandering tribe,—if he had told the savages that the herbs, which every day they trampled underfoot, were endowed with the most potent virtues; that one would restore to health a brother on the verge of death; that another would paralyze into idiocy their wisest sage; that a third would strike lifeless to the dust their most stalwart champion; that tears and laughter, vigor and disease, madness and reason, wakefulness and sleep, existence and dissolution, were coiled up in those unregarded leaves,—would they not have held him a sorcerer or a liar? To half the virtues of the vegetable world mankind are yet in the darkness of the savages I have supposed. There are faculties within us with which certain herbs have affinity, and over which they have power. The moly of the ancients was not all a fable."

One evening, Glyndon had lingered alone and late upon the ramparts,—watching the stars as, one by one, they broke upon the twilight. Never had he felt so sensibly the mighty power of the heavens and the earth upon man! how much the springs of our intellectual being are moved and acted upon by the solemn influences of Nature! As a patient on whom, slowly and by degrees, the agencies of mesmerism are brought to bear, he acknowledged to his heart the growing force of that vast and universal magnetism which is the life of creation, and binds the atom to the whole. A strange and ineffable consciousness of power, of the something great within the perishable clay, appealed to feelings at once dim and glorious,—rather faintly recognized than all unknown. An impulse that he could not resist led him to seek the mystic. He would demand, that hour, his initiation into the worlds beyond our world; he was prepared to breathe a diviner air. He entered the castle, and strode through the shadowy and star-lit gallery which conducted to Mejnour's apartment.

THE END. (1)

(1) So far as Zicci was ever finished.

Edward George Earle Bulwer-Lytton was born on May 25th, 1803 to General William Earle Bulwer and Elizabeth Barbara Lytton, and was the youngest of three sons.

When Edward was four his father died and his mother moved the family to London. As a child he was delicate and neurotic and failed to fit in at any number of boarding schools. However, he was academically and creatively precocious and, as a teenager, he published his first work; Ishmael and Other Poems in 1820.

In 1822 he entered Trinity College, Cambridge, but shortly afterwards moved to Trinity Hall. He continued to write poetry and in 1825 he won the Chancellor's Gold Medal for English verse for Sculpture. The following year he received his B.A. degree and printed, for private circulation, the small volume of poems, Weeds and Wild Flowers.

He appears to have briefly considered a career in the Army and purchased a commission, but sold it without serving.

In August 1827, much against his mother's wishes, he married Rosina Doyle Wheeler, a 25 year old and famous Irish beauty. His mother withdrew his allowance and he was forced to work for a living. The couple had two children, Emily Elizabeth (1828), and Edward Robert (1831) who later became Governor-General and Viceroy of British India (1876–1880).

During his career he was to be extremely prolific and write across a number of genres; historical fiction, mystery, romance, the occult, and science fiction as well as poetry. His personal life style was extravagant but his works sold well enabling him to continue to write in varied styles. Sometimes he would publish anonymously.

In 1828 his novel, Pelham, brought him an income, as well as a commercial and critical reputation. The books intricate plot and humorous, intimate portrayals kept many a gossip busy trying to pair up public figures with characters in the book.

At the time there was a suggestion that it was similar in vein to Benjamin Disraeli's first novel, Vivian Grey, published the previous year. In fact, Bulwer-Lytton admired Disraeli's father, Isaac D'Israeli, who was himself a noted author. Correspondence between them began in the late 1820s and they met for the first time in March 1830, when Isaac D'Israeli dined at Bulwer-Lytton's house. Among the other diners present were Charles Pelham Villiers, who was to enjoy a long parliamentary career, and Alexander Cockburn who would become Lord Chief Justice of England in 1859.

Bulwer-Lytton took a keen interest in and quickly became a follower of Jeremy Bentham, an English philosopher, jurist, and social reformer. Bentham was the founder of modern utilitarianism, which is best described in Bentham's own words as "the sum of all pleasure that results from an action, minus the suffering of anyone involved in the action".

In 1831 Bulwer-Lytton became the editor of the New Monthly magazine but he resigned the following year.

Bulwer-Lytton was elected the Member of Parliament for St Ives in Cornwall, in 1831, after which he was returned for the Lincoln seat in 1832. He sat in Parliament for that city for nine years. He spoke in favour of the Reform Bill, and took the leading part in securing the reduction, after vainly essaying the repeal, of the newspaper stamp duties. His influence was perhaps most keenly felt when, on the Whigs' dismissal from office in 1834, he issued a pamphlet entitled A Letter to a Late Cabinet Minister on the Crisis.

Lord Melbourne, the then Prime Minister, offered Bulwer-Lytton a lordship of the admiralty, which he declined as he had no wish for anything further to deflect him from his writing.

Indeed beginning with the publication of Falkland in 1827 Bulwer-Lytton had kept up a writing schedule that was both prolific and very well received. His income grew as did his reputation.

Bulwer-Lytton reached perhaps the height of his popularity with the publication of Godolphin (1833), followed by The Pilgrims of the Rhine (1834), The Last Days of Pompeii (1834), Rienzi, Last of the Roman Tribunes (1835), and continued until Harold, the Last of the Saxons (1848).

Unfortunately for Bulwer-Lytton his writing and political work had strained his marriage to Rosina. Undoubtedly his infidelity also embittered Rosina and in 1833 they separated acrimoniously with the separation becoming legal in 1836. Three years after that Rosina published Cheveley, or the Man of Honour (1839), a near-libelous fiction bitterly satirising her husband's alleged hypocrisy.

His play Money (1840) was first produced at the Theatre Royal, Haymarket, London, on December 8th, 1840. Its success merited an opening on the other side of the Atlantic and on February 1st, 1841 it opened at the Old Park Theater in New York.

In 1841, he left Parliament and would not return to politics for another 11 years. However that year he started the Monthly Chronicle, a semi-scientific magazine. The Victorian era was filled with many magazines and periodicals all of whom had a great fascination to chronicle and publish the many things that the Empire and Industrial Revolution were discovering, inventing and changing.

The death of Bulwer-Lytton's mother in 1843 was a great sadness to him despite their difference over his marriage. His own "exhaustion of toil and study had been completed by great anxiety and grief", and by "about the January of 1844, I was thoroughly shattered". In his mother's room, Bulwer-Lytton "had inscribed above the mantelpiece a request that future generations preserve the room as his beloved mother had used it"; that request is still essentially honoured to this day.

On 20th February 1844, in accordance with his mother's will, he changed his surname from 'Bulwer' to 'Bulwer-Lytton' and assumed the arms of Lytton by royal licence. His widowed mother had done the same in 1811. But, his brothers would remain plain 'Bulwer'.

Bulwer-Lytton was very interested in the latest medical advances and practices. He happened upon a copy of "Captain Claridge's work on the 'Water Cure', as practised by Priessnitz, at Graefenberg", and "making allowances for certain exaggerations therein", pondered the option of travelling to Graefenberg, but preferred to find something closer to home, with access to his own doctors in case of failure: "I who scarcely lived through a day without leech or potion!"

After reading a pamphlet by Doctor James Wilson, who operated a hydropathic establishment with James Manby Gully at Malvern, he stayed there for "some nine or ten weeks", after which he "continued the system some seven weeks longer under Doctor Weiss, at Petersham", then again at "Doctor Schmidt's magnificent hydropathic establishment at Boppart" (at the former Marienberg Convent at Boppard), after developing a cold and fever upon his return home.

He returned to Parliament in 1852, when, having differed from the policy of Lord John Russell over the Corn Laws, he stood for Hertfordshire as a Conservative, a seat he would now hold until 1866.

In 1858 he entered Lord Derby's government as Secretary of State for the Colonies, thus serving alongside his old friend Disraeli. He took an active interest in the development of the Crown Colony of

British Columbia and wrote with great passion to the Royal Engineers upon assigning them their duties there. The former Hudson Bay's Company Fort Dallas at Camchin, the confluence of the Thompson and Fraser Rivers, was renamed in his honour by Governor Sir James Douglas in 1858 as Lytton, British Columbia.

In June 1858, when her husband was standing as parliamentary candidate for Hertfordshire, his ex-wife Rosina sought him out and denounced him from the crowd. It was humiliating but his actions seemed only to further inflame the situation. He threatened her publishers, withheld her allowance, and denied her access to her children. Finally, he had her committed to a mental asylum. There ensued a public outcry at her treatment and she was released a few weeks later. Rosina chronicled the incident in her memoir, A Blighted Life (1880).

By this time, Bulwer-Lytton's great and prolific literary output was essentially over. He did write a few pieces, now and then usually with a horror or supernatural theme including "The Haunted and the Haunters" or "The House and the Brain" (1859) and a novel, A Strange Story (1862), said to have been an influence for Bram Stoker's Dracula.

When King Otto of Greece abdicated in 1862, Bulwer-Lytton was apparently offered the crown of Greece, which he declined.

In 1866 Bulwer-Lytton was raised to the peerage as Baron Lytton of Knebworth in the County of Hertford but his passion for politics now somewhat dimmed.

The English Rosicrucian society, founded in 1867 by Robert Wentworth Little, claimed Bulwer-Lytton as their 'Grand Patron', but he wrote to the society complaining that he was 'extremely surprised' by their use of the title, as he had 'never sanctioned such'. Nevertheless, a number of esoteric groups continued to claim Bulwer-Lytton as their own, chiefly because some of his writings—such as the 1842 book Zanoni—have included Rosicrucian and other esoteric notions.

Bulwer-Lytton continued to pen several other works, including The Coming Race or Vril: The Power of the Coming Race (1871), which drew heavily on his interest in the occult and contributed to the early growth of the science fiction genre. Its story of a subterranean race waiting to reclaim the surface of the Earth is an early science fiction theme. The book popularised the prevailing Hollow Earth theory. His term "vril" lent its name to Bovril meat extract. Adopted by theosophists and occultists since the 1870s, "vril" would develop into a major esoteric topic, and eventually become closely associated with the ideas of an esoteric neo-Nazism after 1945.

Bulwer-Lytton had long suffered with a disease of the ear and for the last two or three years of his life he lived in Torquay nursing his health.

An operation to cure his deafness resulted in an abscess forming in his ear which later burst.

Edward George Earle Bulwer-Lytton endured intense pain for a week and died at 2am on January 18th, 1873, in Torquay, just short of his 70th birthday. The cause of death was not clear but it was thought at the time that the infection had spread to his brain and caused a fit.

Bulwer-Lytton's last novel was Kenelm Chillingly, which at the time of his death was being serialised in Blackwood's Magazine.

He was buried at Westminster Abbey, though this was against his own wishes.

Among his much-used phrases are "the great unwashed", "pursuit of the almighty dollar", "the pen is mightier than the sword", and the classic opening line "It was a dark and stormy night".

Edward Bulwer-Lytton – A Concise Bibliography

Novels
Falkland (1827)
Pelham: or The Adventures of a Gentleman (1828)
The Disowned (1829)
Devereux (1829)
Paul Clifford (1830)
Eugene Aram (1832)
Godolphin (1833)
The Pilgrims of the Rhine (1834)
The Last Days of Pompeii (1834)
Rienzi, the last of the Roman tribunes (1835)
The Student (1835)
Ernest Maltravers (1837)
Alice, or The Mysteries (1838) A sequel to Ernest Maltravers
Leila: or The Siege of Granada (1838)
Calderon, the Courtier (1838)
Zicci: A Tale (1838)
Night and Morning (1841)
Zanoni (1842)
The Last of the Barons (1843)
Lucretia (1846)
Harold, the Last of the Saxons (1848)
The Caxtons: A Family Picture (1849)
My Novel, or Varieties in English Life (1853)
What Will He Do With It? (1858)
The Haunted and the Haunters or The House and the Brain, a short story (1859)
A Strange Story (1862)
The Coming Race (1871), republished as Vril: The Power of the Coming Race
Kenelm Chillingly (1873)
The Parisians (1873 unfinished)

Verse
Ismael: An Oriental Tale, with Other Poems (1820)
Delmour; or, A Tale of a Sylphid, and Other Poems, (1823)
Sculpture (1825)
Weeds and Wildflowers (1826)
Collected Poems (1831)

The New Timon (1846), an attack on Tennyson published anonymously
King Arthur (1848–9)

The Duchess de la Vallière (1837)
The Lady of Lyons (1838)
The Sea Captain; or, The Birthright [drama], 1839
Richelieu (1839), A five-act play in blank verse
Money (1840)
Not So Bad as We Seem, or, Many Sides to a Character: A Comedy in Five Acts (1851)
The Rightful Heir (1868), based on The Sea Captain
Walpole, or Every Man Has His Price (1869)
Darnley (unfinished)

History of England, (1833)
Letter to a Late Cabinet Minister on the Present Crisis (pamphlet), (1834)
Athens, Its Rise and Fall, (5 Books. Book 1 was published in 1837 and Book 5 posthumously)
A Word to the Public, (1847)
The Odes and Epodes of Horace (Translation), (1869)

www.ingramcontent.com/pod-product-compliance
Lightning Source LLC
Chambersburg PA
CBHW061456170626
46811CB00004B/1532